Mysterious Tales from the Hills

Ruskin Bond is known for his signature simplistic and witty writing style. He is the author of several bestselling short stories, novellas, collections, essays and children's books; and has contributed a number of poems and articles to various magazines and anthologies. At the age of twenty-three, he won the prestigious John Llewellyn Rhys Prize for his first novel, *The Room on the Roof*. He was also the recipient of the Padma Shri in 1999, Lifetime Achievement Award by the Delhi Government in 2012 and the Padma Bhushan in 2014.

Born in 1934, Ruskin Bond grew up in Jamnagar, Shimla, New Delhi and Dehradun. Apart from three years in the UK, he has spent all his life in India, and now lives in Landour, Mussoorie, with his adopted family.

RUSKIN BOND

Mysterious Tales from the Hills

RUPA

Published by
Rupa Publications India Pvt. Ltd 2021
7/16, Ansari Road, Daryaganj
New Delhi 110002

Sales centres:
Bengaluru Chennai
Hyderabad Jaipur Kathmandu
Kolkata Mumbai Prayagraj

Copyright © Ruskin Bond 2021

This is a work of fiction. Names, characters, places and incidents are either the product of the author's imagination or are used fictitiously and any resemblance to any actual person, living or dead, events or locales is entirely coincidental.

All rights reserved.
No part of this publication may be reproduced, transmitted, or stored in a retrieval system, in any form or by any means, electronic, mechanical, photocopying, recording or otherwise, without the prior permission of the publisher.

P-ISBN: 978-93-5520-150-8
E-ISBN: 978-93-5520-151-5

Eleventh impression 2025

15 14 13 12 11

The moral right of the author has been asserted.

Printed in India

This book is sold subject to the condition that it shall not, by way of trade or otherwise, be lent, resold, hired out, or otherwise circulated, without the publisher's prior consent, in any form of binding or cover other than that in which it is published.

CONTENTS

Introduction   *vii*

Miracle at Happy Bazaar	1
A Hill Station Vintage Murders	13
A Case for Inspector Lal	19
He Said It with Arsenic	30
Something in the Water	42
When Darkness Falls	47
A Job Well Done	69
Susanna's Seven Husbands	77
Rhododendrons in the Mist	85
A Mussoorie Mystery	100

INTRODUCTION

When a land is as old as India, with its varied civilizations, rich history and cultural diversity, it's bound to have chockfull of stories and mysteries. These are not just stories of myths and legends, but incidents that involve people who were once residents of these places and have now become somewhat synonymous with the intrigue of the place.

Of course when the land is as old as India, and the stories have gone through generations of telling and re-telling, it's hard to tell what is describing the facts of the incident and what is the storyteller's creative input. But one thing is undisputable; it is these stories (including the varied versions of them that crop up through the generations) that add character to our beloved towns.

This book takes you through tales of unsolved murders—poisoning, cold-blooded stabbing, what have you! It tells the tales of sea creatures that pop up only to swallow young boys, of women who can communicate with the dead, of Sahibs who disappear in their big mansions and of men who only have half faces. This book is for children and adults alike—all you really need is a hankering for a good dose of spookiness!

Ruskin Bond

MIRACLE AT HAPPY BAZAAR

It was called 'Happy' Bus Stop because a local boy called 'Happy', happily drunk, had got into the driver's seat of the local bus and driven it over the edge of the cliff, onto the rocks some seventy feet below the road. Fortunately, the bus had been empty at the time, and only Happy and the vehicle had perished.

When I was a boy, the old road to Tehri had been little more than a footpath, and you walked from one village to the next. If you were in a hurry you could take a ride on a mule—mules could navigate the narrowest of tracks—and reach your destination with a very sore bottom. It was wiser to walk.

Then, in mid-1962–63, after the Chinese incursions, there was a flurry of road-building in the hills, and the old footpaths and mule tracks were turned into motorways. A bus stop came up just outside the Landour boundary, and by 1970 there were buses to Chamba and beyond.

Where there is a bus stop you will find a tea shop, and if the tea shop prospers it will be followed by another tea shop. Then there has to be a vegetable stand, because at the last moment bus passengers will remember to buy vegetables to take home. Sometimes they will fetch seasonal vegetables from their own villages to sell in the Landour market—cucumbers and beans during the monsoon rains, pumpkins and maize a little later. The vegetable stalls near the bus stop and in the town will have fruit and vegetables from all over the country—coconuts and pomegranates, pineapples and custard apples.

As the bus stop grew bigger, and the number of buses increased, the shops prospered. One tea shop specialized in pakoras, the other in samosas; the competition remained friendly.

Soon, a little chemist's shop was opened. After all, there was a hospital nearby, and sometimes the patients, or their relatives, required medicines that were not available from the hospital's small pharmacy. Sick and injured people from the surrounding villages would use the buses to come to the hospital. The town had one ambulance and this was usually engaged in bringing townspeople to the emergency ward. The ambulance had a loud, piercing siren and people living along the main road would be woken up in the middle of the night, or in the early hours before daybreak, by the wail of the ambulance.

Early morning, the first bus left for Chamba. Late evening, the last bus arrived at 'Happy' Bus Stop. Gradually, the owners of the shops expanded their shacks into brick houses. They teetered over the side of the road, packed together like an upside-down Potala Palace.

By the 1990s there were at least ten shops (and residences) near the bus stop, and people began calling it a market. They had forgotten who 'Happy' was, but they called it the Happy Bazaar.

And presently a 'wine' shop opened, to relieve the thirst of bus drivers, passengers, shopkeepers, hospital patients and their relatives, and anyone who cared to stroll down Happy Bazaar. It wasn't strictly a wine shop, merely an outlet for country liquor. If you wanted 'foreign liquor' (i.e. whisky or rum) you had to go to the 'English Wine Shop' in town, where you could get Indian-made foreign liquor.

The country liquor was strong stuff and sometimes fights broke out and accidents took place. An inebriated bus driver tried to take a shortcut to Chamba by avoiding the road altogether, with the result that both he and many of his passengers took a shortcut into their next incarnations.

Fortunately, there was a police outpost not too far away, and things did not get out of hand too often.

All went well for several years, and the population of Happy Bus Stop and Happy Bazaar grew and prospered. They did not pay much attention to the new road that was being built, a bypass that would provide an alternative route into the mountains. And one day, amidst much fanfare, a minister from the state's capital arrived and opened a new bus stop, a couple of miles from Happy Bazaar, and flagged off a brand new bus to Chamba and beyond.

The Happy Bus Stop continued to function—but not for long. The claims of the new bus stop were considered to be much stronger, and it had political backing, which made all the difference. One by one the buses and their crew moved on to the new site. There was a marked decline in the number of people who used the little marketplace. Fruit and vegetables piled up, and the owner of the vegetable stall was kept busy all day, dousing his wares with cold water in order to keep them fresh. One of the tea shops closed down, the owner renting premises at the new site. I remained loyal to the remaining tea shop, as I preferred pakoras to samosas, and, besides, my home was close by.

I sat alone in the tea shop, keeping the owner company.

'Well, at least the mules are back,' said Melaram abruptly. He was always the optimist.

'This was always their road,' I said. 'They resent the cars and buses.'

The muleteers and local villagers helped to make up the loss of business, but it wasn't quite the same; they did not have much money to spend. Occasionally, Melaram would provide tea and pakoras to the relatives of patients who were in the hospital, and this kept him going. And the chemist's shop remained in business, and so did old Abdul the Bulbul (as he was called by the children) who made mattresses and razais for the hospital and local residents. But most of the time Happy Bazaar wore a forlorn look.

And then one day, as I was sitting in the tea shop, contemplating a dish of pakoras, a dapper-looking gentleman walked in and ordered a cup of tea. Melaram and I took notice. It was some time since a stranger had walked into the shop.

Over a glass of hot tea he seemed inclined to talk, although, when we asked him where he came from, he was rather vague and mentioned some town in Kyrgyzstan or Tajikistan, I'm not sure which, and told us his name was Dr Cosmo.

'You can call me Cosmos if you like,' he said with a brilliant smile. 'In reality I belong to the world. To the universe.'

'And what kind of doctor are you?' asked Melaram. 'Can you cure my rheumatism?'

'Of course,' said the stranger. 'But to tell the truth, I'm looking for a quiet place where I can rest from my labours. All this healing can be very taxing. But come closer. Tell me where it hurts. Is there a swelling?'

'In my wrist,' said Melaram. 'And in my elbow. It's worse at night. The pain prevents me from sleeping.'

'Give me your hand.'

Melaram presented his hand, and the stranger took it and held it for some time.

'Do you feel anything?' he asked.

'No.'

The stranger held it a little longer—long enough for me to finish my tea and pakoras.

'I feel a tingling,' said Melaram.

'Good. That's the energy from my body passing into you. It's called cosmic energy. It comes from the sun. It's absorbed by me, and I pass it on to you. You will sleep well tonight. There will be no pain. Now tell me where I can find a place to stay. I like the look of this place. It's restful, at peace with itself.'

'It's restful because most of the people have gone away,' said Melaram. 'This used to be a busy bus stop. But the bus stop was moved closer to the town, and most of our business has gone with it. There's no hotel here. But I have a spare room behind the shop. It used to be occupied by a tailor, but he's moved on too. It's a very simple room—too simple for you, perhaps.'

'The simpler the better,' said Dr Cosmo. 'A good bed, a clean bathroom—and breakfast, perhaps?'

'His parathas are very good,' I chimed in.

'Then lead on, my friend. Show me your honeymoon suite.'

And the next day the good doctor—healer would be a better word—moved in, accompanied by just a few worldly possessions, or rather necessities, and absolutely no medicines or any indication that he was a conventional doctor.

But he liked being called 'doctor', and to one and all he would be known as 'Doctor Cosmos'.

◆

Melaram's rheumatic pains disappeared overnight, and he lost no time in telling his friends and neighbours of his tenant's healing powers. And it didn't take long for others with chronic disabilities to turn up at the tea shop seeking similar treatment.

Dr Cosmos obliged everyone. He laid his hands on

you—on head or heart or back or foot or wherever the patient felt pain or weakness—and then gave the sufferer a few words of encouragement and sent him on his way. Soon people reported that they felt better; some even claimed to be cured. Cripples stood straight and walked with a spring in their step. Old women abandoned their wheelchairs and climbed steep hillsides on foot.

Word of the miraculous healings spread beyond the hill station, and soon the sick and weary from other parts of the land were making their way to Happy Bazaar in search of cures.

Dr Cosmos did not claim to be a faith healer or a dispenser of miracles. It had nothing to do with religion, he said. It was all cosmic energy. It passed through him and into the sufferer, and behold, the pains, the weariness, the ailments disappeared.

'You can try doing it yourself,' he said.

Well, I did try it, but without any success. I tried to cure an old woman's toothache by placing my hand on her cheek, and she brushed it away, saying I was a cheeky fellow and a fraud.

But no one accused Dr Cosmos of being a fraud. Not everyone got better or was returned to normal, but a good many did seem to benefit from his doses of cosmic energy, and he was in great demand. Before long he needed a couple of helpers, and a large room, and these were provided by the bazaar people. They also persuaded him to accept a small fee from his patients to pay for his board and lodging.

A guest house came up to accommodate patients from other towns. It was built where the old bus stop had stood. Nearby hotels and hostelries were reported to be full, even off season. Cars rolled up with rich sufferers, ready to part with large sums of money if they could be cured of chronic ailments, cancer or diabetes or old injuries. And Dr Cosmos treated them too but did not take any 'fees'.

Then some medical men persuaded him to come to Delhi to demonstrate his 'powers', to lecture them on cosmic energy. He made several trips to the capital. He was becoming famous. But every time he returned from Delhi he looked a little thinner, a little more frail, a bit like some of his patients. It was clear that the capital's air or water or atmosphere did not agree with him. He had become accustomed to the good, clean air of the hills.

'Up here, the cosmic energy flows without hindrance,' he claimed.

'Then stay up here,' said Melaram. 'You can't cure all of Delhi of their ailments. I don't go there myself. They should move the capital elsewhere!'

'Someone tried that long ago,' I said. 'They moved to Daulatabad. But it didn't work. I think they missed the dear old Jamuna.'

So Dr Cosmos's trips to Delhi continued, and although his fame grew, his own health deteriorated, so much so that I felt tempted to say, 'Physician, heal thyself.'

When I heard that he had been admitted to one of the capital's premier hospitals, with an 'unknown' and unspecified complaint, I went down to see him, accompanied by Melaram.

Lying there in his hospital bed, he looked desiccated, devoid of life's juices. This was not the Dr Cosmos we knew. He was barely recognizable. His cheeks were sunken, his teeth missing, his hair falling out. But he recognized us, and raised his hand in a feeble greeting.

'What happened to you?' I asked.

He shook his head, whispered: 'I took on too much. Now I have all the diseases in the world. It's a wonderful thing, in a way. Absorbing their fits and fevers, giving them energy in return.'

'Cosmic energy,' I said. 'You should have kept some for yourself.'

He nodded. 'I will recover. I will regain my strength as soon as I am back in the mountains.'

But he did not return to the mountains. Melaram and I had to return without him. He was too far gone. And a week later we heard that he had joined the cosmos. Some of his relatives turned up and buried him in a corner of a

Delhi cemetery; there is no tombstone to mark the place, no record of his fleeting presence on planet earth. No cause of death had been given; but the medical report did mention that traces of strontium had been found in his blood. How did this obscure metallic element get into his system? Had it something to do with the cosmic energy he radiated? We shall never know. There will always be mysteries.

◆

It was thought that the passing of Dr Cosmos would affect the popularity of Happy Bazaar as a destination for tourists. But this did not happen. Curious visitors continued to come our way, many of them eager to see the humble room in which the healer had first seen his patients and sent them happily on their way, bursting with cosmic energy. Some felt that by touching his desk or chair or bed they would obtain relief from their various ailments. And perhaps they did. For thought is a wonderful thing, and mind can prevail over matter.

Happy Bazaar continued to prosper, and so did Melaram, for he owned the premises, and although he did not charge an entry fee, visitors would spend some time in his tea shop, sampling his tea and pakoras. No one made better pakoras.

I was present when a local guide brought a group of

tourists into the shop, and expounded on the history of Happy Bazaar, telling them how it had gained its reputation for happiness because of the miracles performed by the now legendary doctor.

I tried to interrupt and tell them that the bazaar had in fact got its name from the delinquent youth 'Happy' who had driven a bus over a nearby cliff. But no one was listening to me.

A HILL STATION VINTAGE MURDERS

There is less crime in the hills than in the plains, and so the few murders that do take place from time to time stand out as landmarks in the annals of a hill station.

Among the gravestones in the Mussoorie cemetery there is one which bears the inscription: 'Murdered by the hand he befriended.' This is the grave of Mr James Reginald Clapp, a chemist's assistant, who was brutally done to death on the night of 31 August 1909.

Miss Ripley-Bean, who has spent most of her eighty-seven years in this hill station, remembers the case clearly, though she was only a girl at the time. From the details she has given me, and from a brief account in *A Mussoorie Miscellany*, now out of print, I am able to reconstruct this interesting case and a couple of others which were the sensations of their respective 'seasons'.

Mr Clapp was an assistant in the chemist's shop of Messrs. J.B. & E. Samuel (no longer in existence), situated in one of the busiest sections of the Mall. At that time the adjoining cantonment of Landour was an important convalescent centre for British soldiers. Mr Clapp was popular with the soldiers, and he had befriended some of them when they had run short of money. He was a steady worker and sent most of his savings home, to his mother in Birmingham; she was planning to use the money to buy the house in which she lived.

At the time of the murder, Clapp was particularly friendly with a Corporal Allen, who was eventually to be hanged at the Naini Jail. The murder was brutal, the initial attack being launched with a soda-water bottle on the victim's head. Clapp's throat was then cut from ear to ear with his own razor, which was left behind in the room. The body was discovered on the floor of the shop the next morning by the proprietor, Mr Samuel, who did not live on the premises.

Suspicion immediately fell on Corporal Allen because he had left Mussoorie that same night, arriving at Rajpur, in the foothills (a seven-mile walk by the bridle path) many hours later than he was expected at a Rajpur boarding-house. According to some, Clapp had last been seen in the corporal's company.

There was other circumstantial evidence pointing to Allen's guilt. On the day of the murder, Mr Clapp had received his salary, and this sum, in sovereigns and notes, was never traced. Allen was alleged to have made a payment in sovereigns at Rajpur. Someone had given Allen a biscuit tin packed with sandwiches for his journey down, and it was thought that perhaps the tin had been used by the murderer as a safe for the money. But no tin was found, and Allen denied having had one with him.

Allen was arrested at Rajpur and brought back to Mussoorie under escort. He was taken immediately to the victim's bedside, where the body still lay, the police hoping that he might confess his guilt when confronted with the body of the victim; but Allen was unmoved, and protested his innocence.

Meanwhile, other soldiers from among Mr Clapp's friends had collected on the Mall. They had removed their belts and were ready to lynch Allen as soon as he was brought out of the shop. The situation was tense, but further mishap was averted by the resourcefulness of Mr Rust, a photographer, who, being of the same build as the corporal, put on an army coat with a turned-up collar, and arranged to be handcuffed between two policemen. He remained with them inside the shop, in partial view of the mob, while the rest of the police party escorted the corporal out by a back entrance. Mr Rust did not abandon his disguise or leave the shop until word arrived that Allen was secure in the police station.

Corporal Allen was eventually found guilty, and was hanged. But there were many who felt that he had never really been proved guilty, and that he had been convicted on purely circumstantial evidence; and looking back on the case from this distance in time one cannot help feeling that the soldier may have been a victim of circumstances, and perhaps of local prejudice, for he was not liked by his fellows. Allen himself hinted that he was not in the vicinity of the crime that night but in the company of a lady whose integrity he was determined to shield. If this was true, it was a pity that the lady prized her virtue more than her friend's life, for she did not come forward to save him. The chaplain who administered to Allen during his last days in the 'condemned cell' was prepared to absolve the corporal and could not accept that he was a murderer.

One of the hill station's most sensational crimes was committed on 25 July 1927, at the height of the 'season' and in the heart of the town, in Zephyr Hall, then a boarding house. It provided a good deal of excitement for the residents of the boarding house.

Soon after midday, Zephyr Hall residents were startled into brisk activity when a woman screamed and a shot rang out from one of the rooms. Other shots followed in rapid succession.

Those boarders who happened to be in the public lounge or verandah dived for the safety of their rooms; but one unhappy resident, taking the precaution of coming around a corner with his hands held well above his head, ran straight into a levelled pistol. And the man with the gun, who had just killed his wife and wounded his daughter, was still able to see some humour in the situation, for he burst into laughter! The boarder escaped unhurt. But the murderer, Mr Owen, did not savour the situation for long. He shot himself long before the police arrived.

Ten years earlier, on 24 November 1917, another husband had shot his wife.

Mrs Fennimore, the wife of a schoolmaster, had got herself inextricably enmeshed in a defamation law suit, each hearing of which was more distasteful to Mr Fennimore than the previous one. Finally he determined on his own solution. Late at night he armed himself with a loaded revolver, moved to his wife's bedside, and, finding her lying asleep on her side, shot her through the back of the head. For no accountable reason he put the weapon under her pillow, and then completed his plan. Going to the lavatory, three rooms beyond his wife's bedroom, he leaned over his loaded rifle and shot himself.

A CASE FOR INSPECTOR LAL

I met Inspector Keemat Lal about two years ago, while I was living in the hot, dusty town of Shahpur in the plains of northern India.

Keemat Lal had charge of the local police station. He was a heavily built man, slow and rather ponderous, and inclined to be lazy; but, like most lazy people, he was intelligent. He was also a failure. He had remained an inspector for a number of years, and had given up all hopes of a further promotion. His luck was against him, he said. He should never have been a policeman. He had been born under the sign of Capricorn and should really have gone into the restaurant business; but now it was too late to do anything about it.

The Inspector and I had little in common. He was nearing forty, and I was twenty-five. But both of us spoke English, and in Shahpur there were very few people who did. In addition, we were both fond of beer. There were no places of entertainment in Shahpur. The searing heat, the dust that came whirling up from the east, the mosquitoes (almost as numerous as the flies) and the general monotony gave one a thirst for something more substantial than stale lemonade.

My house was on the outskirts of the town, where we were often not disturbed. On two or three evenings in the week, just as the sun was going down and making it possible for one to emerge from the khas-cooled confines of a dark, high-ceilinged bedroom, Inspector Keemat Lal would appear on the verandah steps, mopping the sweat from his face with a small towel, which he used instead of a handkerchief. My only servant, excited at the prospect of serving an inspector of police, would hurry out with glasses, a bucket of ice and several bottles of the best Indian beer.

One evening, after we had overtaken our fourth bottle, I said, 'You must have had some interesting cases in your career, Inspector.'

'Most of them were rather dull,' he said. 'At least the successful ones were. The sensational cases usually went unsolved—otherwise I might have been a superintendent by now. I suppose you are talking of murder cases. Do you remember the shooting of the Minister of the Interior? I was on that one, but it was a political murder and we never solved it.'

'Tell me about a case you solved,' I said. 'An interesting one.' When I saw him looking uncomfortable, I added, 'You don't have to worry, Inspector. I'm a very discreet person, in spite of all the beer I consume.'

'But how can you be discreet? You are a writer.'

I protested: 'Writers are usually very discreet. They always change the names of people and places.'

He gave me one of his rare smiles. 'And how would you describe me, if you were to put me into a story?'

'Oh, I'd leave you as you are. No one would believe in you, anyway.'

He laughed indulgently and poured out more beer. 'I suppose I can change names, too... I will tell you a very interesting case. The victim was an unusual person, and so was the killer. But you must promise not to write this story.'

'I promise,' I lied.

'Do you know Panauli?'

'In the hills? Yes, I have been there once or twice.'

'Good, then you will follow me without my having to be too descriptive. This happened about three years ago, shortly after I had been stationed at Panauli. Nothing much ever happened there. There were a few cases of theft and cheating, and an occasional fight during the summer. A murder took place about once every ten years. It was, therefore, quite an event when the Rani of—was found dead in her sitting room, her head split open by an axe. I knew that I would have to solve the case if I wanted to stay in Panauli.

'The trouble was, anyone could have killed the Rani, and there were some who made no secret of their satisfaction that she was dead. She had been an unpopular woman. Her husband was dead, her children were scattered and her money—for she had never been a very wealthy Rani—had been dwindling away. She lived alone in an old house on the outskirts of the town, ruling the locality with the stern authority of a matriarch. She had a servant, and he was the man who found the body and came to the police, dithering and tongue-tied. I arrested him at once, of course. I knew he was probably innocent, but a basic rule is to grab the first man on the scene of the crime, especially if he happens to be a servant. But we let him go after a beating. There was nothing much he could tell us, and he had a sound alibi.

'The axe with which the Rani had been killed must have been a small woodcutter's axe—so we deduced from the wound. We couldn't find the weapon. It might have been used by a man or a woman, and there were several of both sexes who had a grudge against the Rani. There were bazaar rumours that she had been supplementing her income by trafficking in young women: she had the necessary connections. There were also rumours that she possessed vast wealth, and that it was stored away in her godowns. We did not find any treasure. There were so many rumours darting about like battered shuttlecocks that I decided to stop wasting my time in trying to follow them up. Instead I restricted my enquiries to those people who had been close to the Rani—either in their personal relationships or in actual physical proximity.

'To begin with, there was Mr Kapur, a wealthy businessman from Bombay who had a house in Panauli. He was supposed to be an old admirer of the Rani's. I discovered that he had occasionally lent her money, and that, in spite of his professed friendship for her, he had charged a high rate of interest.

Then there were her immediate neighbours—an American missionary and his wife, who had been trying to convert the Rani to Christianity; an English spinster of seventy who made no secret of the fact that she and the Rani had hated each other with great enthusiasm; a local councillor and his family, who did not get on well with their aristocratic neighbour; and a tailor, who kept his shop close by. None of these people had any powerful motive for killing the Rani—or none that I could discover. But the tailor's daughter interested me.

Her name was Kusum. She was twelve or thirteen years old—a thin dark girl, with lovely black eyes and a swift, disarming smile. While I was making my routine enquiries in the vicinity of the Rani's house, I noticed that the girl always tried to avoid me. When I questioned her about the Rani, and about her own movements on the day of the crime, she pretended to be very vague and stupid.

But I could see she was not stupid, and I became convinced that she knew something unusual about the Rani. She might even know something about the murder. She could have been protecting someone, and was afraid to tell me what she knew. Often, when I spoke to her of the violence of the Rani's death, I saw fear in her eyes. I began to think the girl's life might be in danger, and I had a close watch kept on her. I liked her. I liked her youth and freshness and the innocence and wonder in her eyes. I spoke to her whenever I could, kindly and paternally, and though I knew she rather liked me and found me amusing—the ups and downs of Panauli always left me panting for breath—and though I could see that she *wanted* to tell me something, she always held back at the last moment.

Then, one afternoon while I was in the Rani's house going through her effects, I saw something glistening in a narrow crack near the doorstep. I would not have noticed it if the sun had not been pouring through the window, glinting off the little object. I stooped and picked up a piece of glass. It was part of a broken bangle.

I turned the fragment over in my hand. There was something familiar about its colour and design. Didn't Kusum wear similar glass bangles? I went to look for the girl but she was not at her father's shop. I was told that she had gone down the hill to gather firewood.

I decided to take the narrow path down the hill. It went round some rocks and cactus, and then disappeared into a forest of oak trees. I found Kusum sitting at the edge of the forest, a bundle of twigs beside her.

"You are always wandering about alone," I said. "Don't you feel afraid?"

"It is safer when I am alone," she replied. "Nobody comes here."

I glanced quickly at the bangles on her wrist, and noticed that their colour matched that of the broken piece. I held out the bit of broken glass and said, "I found it in the Rani's house. It must have fallen…"

She did not wait for me to finish what I was saying. With a look of terror, she sprang up from the grass and fled into the forest.

I was completely taken aback. I had not expected such a reaction. Of what significance was the broken bangle? I hurried after the girl, slipping on the smooth pine needles that covered the slopes. I was searching amongst the trees when I heard someone sobbing behind me. When I turned round, I saw the girl standing on a boulder, facing me with an axe in her hands.

When Kusum saw me staring at her, she raised the axe and rushed down the slope towards me.

I was too bewildered to be able to do anything but stare with open mouth as she rushed at me with the axe. The impetus of her run would have brought her right up against me, and the axe, coming down, would probably have crushed my skull, thick though it is. But while she was still six feet from me, the axe flew out of her hands. It sprang into the air as though it had a life of its own and came curving towards me.

In spite of my weight, I moved swiftly aside. The axe grazed my shoulder and sank into the soft bark of the tree behind me. And Kusum dropped at my feet, weeping hysterically.'

Inspector Keemat Lal paused in order to replenish his glass. He took a long pull at the beer, and the froth glistened on his moustache.

'And then what happened?' I prompted him.

'Perhaps it could only have happened in India—and to a person like me,' he said. 'This sudden compassion for the person you are supposed to destroy. Instead of being furious and outraged, instead of seizing the girl and marching her off to the police station, I stroked her head and said silly comforting things.'

'And she told you that she had killed the Rani?'

'She told me how the Rani had called her to her house and given her tea and sweets. Mr Kapur had been there. After some time he began stroking Kusum's arms and squeezing her knees. She had drawn away, but Kapur kept pawing her. The Rani was telling Kusum not to be afraid, that no harm would come to her. Kusum slipped away from the man and made a rush for the door. The Rani caught her by the shoulders and pushed her back into the room. The Rani was getting angry. Kusum saw the axe lying in a corner of the room. She seized it, raised it above her head and threatened Kapur. The man realized that he had gone too far, and, valuing his neck, backed away. But the Rani, in a great rage, sprang at the girl. And Kusum, in desperation and panic, brought the axe down across the Rani's head.

The Rani fell to the ground. Without waiting to see what Kapur might do, Kusum fled from the house. Her bangle must have broken when she stumbled against the door. She ran into the forest and, after concealing the axe amongst some tall ferns, lay weeping on the grass until it grew dark. But such was her nature, and such the resilience of youth, that she recovered sufficiently to be able to return home looking her normal self. And during the following days she managed to remain silent about the whole business.'

'What did you do about it?' I asked.

Keemat Lal looked me straight in my beery eye.

'Nothing,' he said. 'I did absolutely nothing. I couldn't have the girl put away in a remand home. It would have crushed her spirit.'

'And what about Kapur?'

'Oh, he had his own reasons for remaining quiet, as you may guess. No, the case was closed—or perhaps I should say the file was put in my pending tray. My promotion, too, went into the pending tray.'

'It didn't turn out very well for you,' I said.

'No. Here I am in Shahpur, and still an inspector. But, tell me, what would you have done if you had been in my place?'

I considered his question carefully for a moment or two, then said, 'I suppose it would have depended on how much sympathy the girl evoked in me. She had killed in innocence…'

'Then you would have put your personal feelings above your duty to uphold the law?'

'Yes. But I would not have made a very good policeman.'

'Exactly.'

'Still, it's a pity that Kapur got off so easily.'

'There was no alternative if I was to let the girl go. But he didn't get off altogether. He found himself in trouble later for swindling some manufacturing concern, and went to jail for a couple of years.'

'And the girl—did you see her again?'

'Well, before I was transferred from Panauli, I saw her occasionally on the road. She was usually on her way to school. She would greet me with joined palms, and call me Uncle.'

The beer bottles were all empty, and Inspector Keemat Lal got up to leave. His final words to me were, 'I should never have been a policeman.'

HE SAID IT WITH ARSENIC

Is there such a person as a born murderer—in the sense that there are born writers and musicians, born winners and losers? One can't be sure. The urge to do away with troublesome people is common to most of us, but only a few succumb to it.

If ever there was a born murderer, he must surely have been William Jones. The thing came so naturally to him. No extreme violence, no messy shootings or hackings or throttling; just the right amount of poison, administered with skill and discretion.

A gentle, civilized sort of person was Mr Jones. He

He Said It with Arsenic

collected butterflies and arranged them systematically in glass cases. His ether bottle was quick and painless. He never stuck pins into the beautiful creatures.

Have you ever heard of the Agra Double Murder? It happened, of course, a great many years ago, when Agra was a far-flung outpost of the British Empire. In those days, William Jones was a male nurse in one of the city's hospitals. The patients—especially terminal cases—spoke highly of the care and consideration he showed them. While most nurses, both male and female, preferred to attend to the more hopeful cases, nurse William was always prepared to stand duty over a dying patient.

He felt a certain empathy for the dying; he liked to see them on their way. It was just his good nature, of course.

On a visit to nearby Meerut, he met and fell in love with Mrs Browning, the wife of the local station-master. Impassioned love letters were soon putting a strain on the Agra–Meerut postal service. The envelopes grew heavier—not so much because the letters were growing longer but because they contained little packets of a powdery white substance, accompanied by detailed instructions as to its correct administration.

Mr Browning, an unassuming and trustful man—one of the world's born losers, in fact—was not the sort to read his wife's correspondence. Even when he was seized by frequent attacks of colic, he put them clown to an impure water supply. He recovered from one bout of vomitting and diarrohea only to be racked by another.

He was hospitalized on a diagnosis of gastroenteritis; and, thus freed from his wife's ministrations, soon got better. But on returning home and drinking a glass of nimbu paani brought to him by the solicitous Mrs Browning, he had a relapse from which he did not recover.

Those were the days when deaths from cholera and related diseases were only too common in India, and death certificates were easier to obtain than dog licences.

After a short interval of mourning (it was the hot weather and you couldn't wear black for long), Mrs Browning moved to Agra, where she rented a house next door to William Jones.

I forgot to mention that Mr Jones was also married. His wife was an insignificant creature, no match for a genius like William. Before the hot weather was over, the dreaded cholera had taken her too. The way was clear for the lovers to unite in holy matrimony.

But Dame Gossip lived in Agra too, and it was not long before tongues were wagging and anonymous letters were being received by the Superintendent of Police. Enquiries were instituted. Like most infatuated lovers, Mrs Browning had hung on to her beloved's letters and billet-doux, and these soon came to light. The silly woman had kept them in a box beneath her bed.

Exhumations were ordered in both Agra and Meerut. Arsenic keeps well, even in the hottest of weather, and there was no dearth of it in the remains of both victims.

Mr Jones and Mrs Browning were arrested and charged with murder.

'Is Uncle Bill really a murderer?' I asked from the living-room sofa in my grandmother's house in Dehra. (It's time that I told you that William Jones was my uncle, my mother's half-brother.)

I was eight or nine at the time. Uncle Bill had spent the previous summer with us in Dehra and had stuffed me with bazaar sweets and pastries, all of which I had consumed without suffering any ill effects.

'Who told you that about Uncle Bill?' asked Grandmother.

'I heard it in school. All the boys were asking me the same question—"Is your uncle a murderer?" They say he poisoned both his wives.'

'He had only one wife,' snapped Aunt Mabel.

'Did he poison her?'

'No, of course not. How can you say such a thing!'

'Then why is Uncle Bill in gaol?'

'Who says he's in gaol?'

'The boys at school. They heard it from their parents. Uncle Bill is to go on trial in the Agra fort.'

There was a pregnant silence in the living room, then Aunt Mabel burst out: 'It was all that awful woman's fault.'

'Do you mean Mrs Browning?' asked Grandmother.

'Yes, of course. She must have put him up to it. Bill couldn't have thought of anything so-so diabolical!'

'But he sent her the powder, clear. And don't forget—Mrs Browning has since…'

Grandmother stopped in mid-sentence, and both she and Aunt Mabel glanced surreptitiously at me.

'Committed suicide,' I filled in. 'There was still some powder with her.'

Aunt Mabel's eyes rolled heavenwards. 'This boy is impossible. I don't know what he will be like when he grows up.'

'At least I won't be like Uncle Bill,' I said. 'Fancy poisoning people! If I kill anyone, it will be in a fair fight. I suppose they'll hang Uncle?'

'Oh, I hope not!'

Grandmother was silent. Uncle Bill was her stepson, but she did have a soft spot for him. Aunt Mabel, his sister, thought he was wonderful. I had always considered him to be a bit soft but had to admit that he was generous. I tried to imagine him dangling at the end of a hangman's rope, but somehow he didn't fit the picture.

As things turned out, he wasn't hung. White people in

He Said It with Arsenic

India seldom got the death sentence, although the hangman was pretty busy disposing off dacoits and political terrorists. Uncle Bill was given a life sentence and settled down to a sedentary job in the prison library at Naini, near Allahabad. His gifts as a male nurse went unappreciated; they did not trust him in the hospital.

He was released after seven or eight years, shortly after the country became an Independent Republic. He came out of gaol to find that the British were leaving, either for England or the remaining colonies. Grandmother was dead. Aunt Mabel and her husband had settled in South Africa. Uncle Bill realized that there was little future for him in India and followed his sister out to Johannesburg. I was in my last year at boarding school. After my father's death, my mother had married an Indian, and now my future lay in India.

I did not see Uncle Bill after his release from prison, and no one dreamt that he would ever turn up again in India.

In fact, fifteen years were to pass before he came back, and by then I was in my early thirties, the author of a book that had become something of a bestseller. The previous fifteen years had been a struggle—the sort of struggle that every young freelance writer experiences—but at last the hard work was paying off and the royalties were beginning to come in.

I was living in a small cottage on the outskirts of the

hill station of Fosterganj, working on another book, when I received an unexpected visitor.

He was a thin, stooped, grey-haired man in his late fifties, with a straggling moustache and discoloured teeth. He looked feeble and harmless but for his eyes which were pale, cold blue. There was something slightly familiar about him.

'Don't you remember me? He asked. Not that I really expect you to, after all these years...'

'Wait a minute. Did you teach me at school?'

'No—but you're getting warm.' He put his suitcase down and I glimpsed his name on the airlines label. I looked up in astonishment. 'You're not—you couldn't be...'

'Your Uncle Bill,' he said with a grin and extended his hand. 'None other!' And he sauntered into the house.

I must admit that I had mixed feelings about his arrival. While I had never felt any dislike for him, I hadn't exactly approved of what he had done. Poisoning, I felt, was a particularly reprehensible way of getting rid of inconvenient people: not that I could think of any commendable ways of getting rid of them! Still, it had happened a long time ago, he'd been punished, and presumably he was a reformed character.

'And what have you been doing all these years?' he asked me, easing himself into the only comfortable chair in the room.

'Oh just writing,' I said.

'Yes, I heard about your last book. It's quite a success, isn't it?'

'It's doing quite well. Have you read it?'

'I don't do much reading.'

'And what have you been doing all these years, Uncle Bill?'

'Oh, knocking about here and there. Worked for a soft drink company for some time. And then with a drug firm. My knowledge of chemicals was useful.'

'Weren't you with Aunt Mabel in South Africa?'

'I saw quite a lot of her, until she died a couple of years ago. Didn't you know?'

'No. I've been out of touch with relatives.' I hoped he'd take that as a hint. 'And what about her husband?'

'Died too, not long after. Not many of us left, my boy. That's why, when I saw something about you in the papers, I thought—why not go and seem my only nephew again?'

'You're welcome to stay a few days,' I said quickly. 'Then I have to go to Bombay.' (This was a lie, but I did not relish the prospect of looking after Uncle Bill for the rest of his days.)

'Oh, I won't be staying long,' he said. 'I've got a bit of money put by in Johannesburg. It's just that—so far as I know—you're my only living relative, and I thought it would be nice to see you again.'

Feeling relieved, I set about trying to make Uncle Bill as comfortable as possible. I gave him my bedroom and turned the window-seat into a bed for myself. I was a hopeless cook but, using all my ingenuity, I scrambled some eggs for supper. He waved aside my apologies; he'd always been a frugal eater, he said. Eight years in gaol had given him a cast-iron stomach.

He did not get in my way but left me to my writing and my lonely walks. He seemed content to sit in the spring sunshine and smoke his pipe.

It was during our third evening together that he said, 'Oh, I almost forgot. There's a bottle of sherry, in my suitcase. I brought it especially for you.'

'That was very thoughtful of you, Uncle Bill. How did you know I was fond of sherry?'

'Just my intuition. You do like it, don't you?'

'There's nothing like a good sherry.'

He went to his bedroom and came back with an unopened bottle of South African sherry.

'Now you just relax near the fire,' he said agreeably. 'I'll open the bottle and fetch glasses.'

He went to the kitchen while I remained near the electric fire, flipping through some journals. It seemed to me that Uncle Bill was taking rather a long time. Intuition must be a family trait, because it came to me quite suddenly—the thought that Uncle Bill might be intending to poison me.

After all, I thought, here he is after nearly fifteen years, apparently for purely sentimental reasons. But I had just published a bestseller. And I was his nearest relative. If I was to die, Uncle Bill could lay claim to my estate and probably live comfortably on my royalties for the next five or six years!

What had really happened to Aunt Mabel and her husband, I wondered. And where did Uncle Bill get the money for a flight ticket to India?

Before I could ask myself any more questions, he reappeared with the glasses on a tray. He set the tray on a small table that stood between us. The glasses had been filled. The sherry sparkled.

I stared at the glass nearest me, trying to make out if the liquid in it was cloudier than that in the other glass. But there appeared to be no difference.

I decided I would not take any chances. It was a round tray, made of smooth Kashmiri walnut wood. I turned it round with lily index finger, so that the glasses changed places.

'Why did you do that?' asked Uncle Bill.

'It's a custom in these parts. You turn the tray with the sun, a complete revolution. It brings good luck.'

Uncle Bill looked thoughtful for a few moments, then said, 'Well, let's have some more luck,' and turned the tray around again.

'Now you've spoilt it,' I said. 'You're not supposed to keep revolving it! That's bad luck. I'll have to turn it about again to cancel out the bad luck.'

The tray swung round once more, and Uncle Bill had the glass that was meant for me.

'Cheers!' I said, and drank from my glass.

It was good sherry.

Uncle Bill hesitated. Then he shrugged, said 'Cheers', and drained his glass quickly.

But he did not offer to fill the glasses again.

Early next morning he was taken violently ill. I heard him retching in his room, and I got up and went to see if there was anything I could do. He was groaning, his head hanging over the side of the bed. I brought him a basin and a jug of water.

'Would you like me to fetch a doctor?' I asked.

He shook his head. 'No, I'll be all right. It must be something I ate.'

'It's probably the water. It's not too good at this time of the year. Many people come down with gastric trouble during their first few days in Fosterganj.'

'Ah, that must be it,' he said, and doubled up as a fresh spasm of pain and nausea swept over him.

He was better by evening—whatever had gone into the glass must have been by way of the preliminary dose and a day later he was well enough to pack his suitcase and announce his departure. The climate of Fosterganj did not agree with him, he told me.

Just before he left, I said; 'Tell me, Uncle, why did you drink it?'

'Drink what? The water?'

'No, the glass of sherry into which you'd slipped one of your famous powder.'

He gaped at me, then gave a nervous whinnying laugh. 'You will have your little joke, won't you?'

'No, I mean it,' I said. 'Why did you drink the stuff? It was meant for me, of course.'

He looked down at his shoes, then gave a little shrug and turned away.

'In the circumstances,' he said, 'it seemed the only decent thing to do.'

I'll say this for Uncle Bill: he was always the perfect gentleman.

SOMETHING IN THE WATER

I discovered the pool near Rajpur on a hot summer's day some fifteen years ago. It was shaded by close-growing sal trees, and looked cool and inviting. I took off my clothes and dived in.

The water was colder than I had expected. It was an icy glacial cold. The sun never touched it for long, I supposed. Striking out vigorously, I swam to the other end of the pool and pulled myself up on the rocks, shivering.

But I wanted to swim some more. So I dived in again and did a gentle breaststroke towards the middle of the pool. Something slid between my legs. Something slimy, pulpy. I could see no one, hear nothing. I swam away, but the slippery floating thing followed me. I did not like it. Something curled around my leg. Not an underwater plant. Something that sucked at my foot. A long tongue licked my calf. I struck out wildly, thrust myself away from whatever it was that sought my company. Something lonely, lurking in the shadows. Kicking up spray, I swam like a frightened porpoise fleeing from some terror of the deep.

Safely out of the water, I found a warm, sunny rock and stood there looking down at the water.

Nothing stirred. The surface of the pool was now calm and undisturbed, just a few fallen leaves floating around. Not a frog, not a fish, not a waterbird in sight. And that in itself seemed strange. For you would have expected some sort of pond life to have been in evidence.

But something lived in the pool, of that I was sure. Something very cold-blooded, colder and wetter than the water. Could it have been a corpse trapped in the weeds? I did not want to know; so I dressed and hurried away.

A few days later I left for Delhi, where I went to work in an ad agency, telling people how to beat the summer heat by drinking fizzy drinks that made you more thirsty. The pool in the forest was forgotten.

It was ten years before I visited Rajpur again. Leaving the small hotel where I was staying, I found myself walking through the same old sal forest, drawn almost irresistibly towards the pool where I had not been able to finish my swim. I was not overeager to swim there again, but I was curious to know if the pool still existed.

Well, it was there all right, although the surroundings had changed and a number of new houses and other buildings had come up where formerly there had only been wilderness. And there was a fair amount of activity in the vicinity of the pool.

A number of labourers were busy with buckets and rubber pipes, draining water from the pool. They had also dammed off and diverted the little stream that fed it.

Overseeing this operation was a well-dressed man in a white safari suit. I thought at first that he was an honorary forest warden, but it turned out that he was the owner of a new school that had been set up nearby.

'Do you live in Rajpur?' he asked.

'I used to... Once upon a time... Why are you emptying the pool?'

'It's become a hazard,' he said. 'Two of my boys were drowned here recently. Both senior students. Of course, they weren't supposed to be swimming here without permission, the pool is off-limits. But you know what boys are like. Make a rule and they feel duty-bound to break it.'

He told me his name was Kapoor, and led me back to his

house, a newly built bungalow with a wide, cool verandah. His servant brought us glasses of cold sherbet. We sat in cane chairs overlooking the pool and the forest. Across a clearing, a gravelled road led to the school buildings, newly whitewashed and glistening in the sun.

'Were the boys there at the same time?' I asked.

'Yes, they were friends. And they must have been attacked by absolute fiends. Limbs twisted and broken, faces disfigured. But death was due to drowning—that was the verdict of the medical examiner.'

We gazed down at the shallows of the pool, where a couple of men were still at work, the others having gone for their midday meal.

'Perhaps it would be better to leave the place alone,' I said. 'Put a barbed wire fence around it. Keep your boys away. Thousands of years ago, this valley was an inland sea. A few small pools and streams are all that is left of it.'

'I want to fill it in and build something there. An open-air theatre, maybe. We can always create an artificial pond somewhere else.'

Presently only one man remained at the pool, knee-deep in muddy churned-up water. And Mr Kapoor and I both saw what happened next.

Something rose out of the bottom of the pool. It looked like a giant snail, but its head was part-human, its body and limbs part-squid or -octopus. An enormous succubus. It stood taller than the man in the pool. A creature soft and slimy, a survivor from our primeval past.

With a great sucking motion, it enveloped the man completely so that only his arms and legs could be seen thrashing about wildly and futilely. The succubus dragged him down under the water.

Kapoor and I left the verandah and ran to the edge of the pool. Bubbles rose from the green scum near the surface. All was still and silent. And then, like bubblegum issuing from the mouth of a child, the mangled body of the man shot out of the water and came spinning towards us.

Dead and drowned and sucked dry of its fluids.

Naturally no more work was done at the pool. The story was put out that the labourer had slipped and fallen to his death on the rocks. Kapoor swore me to secrecy. His school would have to close down if there were too many strange drownings and accidents in its vicinity. But he walled the place off from his property and made it practically inaccessible. The dense undergrowth of the sal forest now hides the approach.

The monsoon rains came and the pool filled up again.

I can tell you how to get there if you'd like to see it. But I wouldn't advise you to go for a swim.

WHEN DARKNESS FALLS

Markham had, for many years, lived alone in a small room adjoining the disused cellars of the old Empire Hotel in one of our hill stations. His army pension gave him enough money to pay for his room rent and his basic needs, but he shunned the outside world—by daylight, anyway—partly because of a natural reticence and partly because he wasn't very nice to look at.

While Markham was serving in Burma during the War, a shell had exploded near his dugout, tearing away most of his face. Plastic surgery was then in its infancy, and although the doctors had done their best, even going to the extent of giving Markham a false nose, his features were permanently ravaged. On the few occasions that he had walked abroad by day, he had been mistaken for someone in the final stages of leprosy and been given a wide berth.

He had been given the basement room by the hotel's elderly estate manager, Negi, who had known Markham in the years before the War, when Negi was just a room-boy. Markham had himself been a youthful assistant manager at the time, and he had helped the eager young Negi advance from room-boy to bartender to office clerk. When Markham took up a wartime commission, Negi rose even further. Now Markham was well into his late sixties, with Negi not very far behind. After a post-War, post-Independence slump, the hill station was thriving again; but both Negi and Markham belonged to another era, another time and place. So did the old hotel, now going to seed, but clinging to its name and surviving on its reputation.

'We're dead, but we won't lie down,' joked Markham, but he didn't find it very funny.

Day after day, alone in the stark simplicity of his room, there was little he could do except read or listen to his short-wave transistor radio; but he would emerge at night to prowl about the vast hotel grounds and occasionally take a midnight stroll along the deserted Mall.

During these forays into the outer world, he wore an

old felt hat, which hid part of his face. He had tried wearing a mask, but that had been even more frightening for those who saw it, especially under a street lamp. A couple of honeymooners, walking back to the hotel late at night, had come face to face with Markham and had fled the hill station the next day. Dogs did not like the mask, either. They set up a furious barking at Markham's approach, stopping only when he removed the mask; they did not seem to mind his face. A policeman returning home late had accosted Markham, suspecting him of being a burglar, and snatched off the mask. Markham, sans nose, jaw and one eye, had smiled a crooked smile, and the policeman had taken to his heels. Thieves and goondas he could handle; not ghostly apparitions straight out of hell.

Apart from Negi, only a few knew of Markham's existence. These were the lower-paid employees who had grown used to him over the years, as one gets used to a lame dog or a crippled cow. The gardener, the sweeper, the dhobi, the night chowkidar, all knew him as a sort of presence. They did not look at him. A man with one eye is said to have the evil eye; and one baleful glance from Markham's single eye was enough to upset anyone with a superstitious nature. He had no problems with the menial staff, and he wisely kept away from the hotel lobby, bar, dining room and corridors—he did not want to frighten the customers away; that would have spelt an end to his own liberty. The owner, who was away most of the time, did not know of his existence; nor did his wife, who lived in the east wing of the hotel, where Markham had never ventured.

The hotel covered a vast area, which included several unused buildings and decaying outhouses. There was a beer garden, no longer frequented, overgrown with weeds and untamed shrubbery. There were tennis courts, rarely used; a squash court, inhabited by a family of goats; a children's playground with a broken see-saw; a ballroom which hadn't seen a ball in fifty years; cellars which were never opened; and a billiard room, said to be haunted.

As his name implied, Markham's forebears were English, with a bit of Allahabad thrown in. It was said that he was related to Kipling on his mother's side; but he never made this claim himself. He had fair hair and one grey-blue eye. The other, of course, was missing.

His artificial nose could be removed whenever he wished, and as he found it a little uncomfortable he usually took it off when he was alone in his room. It rested on his bedside table, staring at the ceiling. Over the years it had acquired a character of its own, and those (like Negi) who had seen it looked upon it with a certain amount of awe. Markham avoided looking at himself in the mirror, but sometimes he had to shave one side of his face, which included a few surviving teeth. There was a gaping hole in his left cheek. And after all these years, it still looked raw.

◆

When it was past midnight, Markham emerged from his lair and prowled the grounds of the old hotel. They belonged to him, really, as no one else patrolled them at that hour—not even the night chowkidar, who was usually to be found asleep on a tattered sofa outside the lounge.

Wearing his old hat and cape, Markham did his rounds. He was a ghostly figure, no doubt, and the few who had glimpsed him in those late hours had taken him for a supernatural visitor. In this way the hotel had acquired a reputation of being haunted. Some guests liked the idea of having a resident ghost; others stayed away.

On this particular night Markham was more restless than usual, more discontented with himself in particular and with the world in general; he wanted a little change—and who wouldn't in similar circumstances?

He had promised Negi that he would avoid the interior of the hotel as far as possible; but it was midsummer—the days were warm and languid, the nights cool and balmy—and he felt like being in the proximity of other humans even if he could not socialize with them.

And so, late at night, he slipped out of the passage to his cellar room and ascended the steps that led to the old banquet hall, now just a huge dining room. A single light was burning at the end of the hall. Beneath it stood an old piano.

Markham lifted the lid and ran his fingers over the keys. He could still pick out a tune, although it was many years since he had played for anyone or even for himself. Now at least he could indulge himself a little. An old song came back to him, and he played it softly, hesitantly, recalling a few words:

> But it's a long, long time, from May to December,
> And the days grow short when we reach
> September...

He couldn't remember all the words, so he just hummed a little as he played. Suddenly, something came down with a crash at the other end of the room. Markham looked up, startled. The hotel cat had knocked over a soup tureen that had been left on one of the tables. Seeing Markham's tall, shifting shadow on the wall, its hair stood on end. And with a long, low wail it fled the banquet room.

Markham left too, and made his way up the carpeted staircase to the first-floor corridor.

Not all the rooms were occupied. They seldom were these

days. He tried one or two doors, but they were locked. He walked to the end of the passage and tried the last door. It was open.

Assuming the room was unoccupied, he entered it quietly. The lights were off, but there was sufficient moonlight coming through the large bay window with its view of the mountains. Markham looked towards the large double bed and saw that it was occupied. A young couple lay there, fast asleep, wrapped in each other's arms. A touching sight! Markham smiled bitterly. It was over forty years since anyone had lain in his arms.

There were footsteps in the passage. Someone stood outside the closed door. Had Markham been seen prowling about the corridors? He moved swiftly to the window, unlatched it, and stepped quickly out on to the landing abutting the roof. Quietly he closed the window and moved away.

Outside, on the roof, he felt an overwhelming sense of freedom. No one would find him there. He wondered why he hadn't thought of the roof before. Being on it gave him a feeling of ownership. The hotel, and all who lived in it, belonged to him.

The lights, from a few skylights and the moon above, helped him to move unhindered over the sloping, corrugated old tin roof. He looked out at the mountains, striding away into the heavens. He felt at one with them.

The owner, Mr Khanna, was away on one of his extended trips abroad. Known to his friends as the Playboy of the Western World, he spent a great deal of his time and money in foreign capitals: London, Paris, New York, Amsterdam. Mr Khanna's wife had health problems (mostly in her mind) and seldom travelled, except to visit godmen and faith healers. At this point in time she was suffering from insomnia, and was pacing about her room in her dressing gown, a loose-fitting garment that did little to conceal her overblown figure; for inspite of her many ailments, her appetite for everything on the menu card was undiminished. Right now she was looking for her Sleeping tablets. Where on earth had she put them? They were not on her bedside table; not, on the dressing table; not on the bathroom shelf. Perhaps they were in her handbag. She rummaged through a drawer, found and opened the bag, and extracted a strip of Valium. Pouring herself a glass of water from the bedside carafe, she tossed her head back, revealing several layers of chin. Before she could swallow the tablet, she saw a face at the skylight. Not really a face. Not a human face, that is. An empty eye socket, a wicked grin and a nose that wasn't a nose, pressed flat against the glass.

Mrs Khanna sank to the floor and passed out. She had no need of the sleeping tablet that night.

When Darkness Falls

◆

For the next couple of days Mrs Khanna was quite hysterical and spoke wildly of a wolf-man or rakshas who was pursuing her. But no one—not even Negi—attributed the apparition to Markham, who had always avoided the guests' rooms.

The daylight hours he passed in his cellar room, which received only a dapple of late afternoon sunlight through a narrow aperture that passed for a window. For about ten minutes the sun rested on a framed picture of Markham's mother, a severe-looking but handsome woman who must have been in her forties when the picture was taken. His father, an army captain, had been killed in the trenches at Mons during the First World War. His picture stood there, too; a dashing figure in uniform. Sometimes Markham wished that he, too, had died from his wounds; but he had been kept alive, and then he had stayed dead-alive all these years, a punishment maybe for sins and excesses committed in some former existence. Perhaps there was something in the theory or belief in karma, although he wished that things would even out a little more in this life—why did we have to wait for the next time around? Markham had read Emerson's essay on the law of compensation, but that didn't seem to work either. He had often thought of suicide as a way of cheating the fates that had made him, the child of handsome parents, no better than a hideous gargoyle; but he had thrust the thought aside, hoping (as most of us do) that things would change for the better.

His room was tidy—it had the bare necessities—and those pictures were the only mementoes of a past he couldn't forget. He had his books, too, for he considered them necessities—the Greek philosophers, Epicurus, Epictetus, Marcus Aurelius, Seneca. When Seneca had nothing left to live for, he had cut his wrists in his bathtub and bled slowly to death. Not a bad way to go, thought Markham; except that he didn't have a bathtub, only a rusty iron bucket.

Food was left outside his door, as per instructions; sometimes fresh fruit and vegetables, sometimes a cooked meal. If there was a wedding banquet in the hotel, Negi would remember to send Markham some roast chicken or pilaf. Markham looked forward to the marriage season with its lavish wedding parties. He was a permanent though unknown wedding guest.

After discovering the freedom of the Empire's roof, Markham's nocturnal excursions seldom went beyond the hotel's sprawling estate. As sure-footed as when he was a soldier, he had no difficulty in scrambling over the decaying rooftops, moving along narrow window ledges, and leaping from one landing or balcony to another. It was late summer, and guests often left their windows open to enjoy the pine-scented breeze that drifted over the hillside. Markham was no voyeur, he was really too insular and subjective a person for that form of indulgence; nevertheless, he found it fascinating to observe people in their unguarded moments: how they preened in front of mirrors, of talked to themselves, or attended to their little vanities, or sang or scratched or made love (or tried to), or drank themselves into a stupor. There were many men (and a few women) who preferred drinking in their rooms to drinking in the bar—it was cheaper, and they could get drunk and stupid without making fools of themselves in public.

One of those who enjoyed a quiet tipple in her room was Mrs Khanna. A vodka with tomato juice was her favourite drink. Markham was watching her soak up her third Bloody Mary when the room telephone rang and Mrs Khanna, receiving some urgent message, left her room and went swaying down the corridor like a battleship of yore.

On an impulse, Markham slipped in through the open window and crossed the room to the table where the bottles were arranged. He felt like having a Bloody Mary himself. It was years since he'd had one; not since that evening at New Delhi's Imperial, when he was on his first leave. Now a little rum during the winter months was his only indulgence.

Taking a clean glass, he poured himself three fingers of vodka and drank it neat. He was about to pour himself another drink when Mrs Khanna entered the room. She stood frozen in her tracks. For there stood the creature of her previous nightmare, the half-face wolf-demon, helping himself to her vodka!

Mrs Khanna screamed. And screamed again.

Markham made a quick exit through the window and vanished into the night. But Mrs Khanna would not stop screaming—not until Negi, half the staff and several guests had entered the room to try and calm her down.

◆

Commotion reigned for a couple of days. Doctors came and went. Policemen came and went. So did Mrs Khanna's palpitations. She insisted that the hotel be searched for the maniac who was in hiding somewhere, only emerging from his lair to single her out for attention. Negi kept the searchers away from the cellar, but he went down himself and confronted Markham.

'Mr Markham, sir, you must keep away from the rooms and the main hotel. Mrs Khanna is very upset. She's called in the police and she's having the hotel searched.'

'I'm sorry, Mr Negi, I did not mean to frighten anyone. It's just that I get restless down here.'

'If she finds out you're living here, you'll have to go.

She gives the orders when Mr Khanna is away.'

'This is my only home. Where would I go?'

'I know, Mr Markham, I know. I understand. But do others? It unnerves them, coming upon you without any warning. Stories are going around . . . Business is bad enough without the hotel getting a reputation for strange goings-on. If you must go out at night, use the rear gate and stick to the forest path. Avoid the Mall road. Times have changed, Mr Markham. There are no private places any more. If you have to leave, you will be in the public eye—and I know you don't want that...'

'No, I can't leave this place. I'll stick to my room. You've been good to me, Mr Negi.'

'That's all right. I'll see that you get what you need. Just keep out of sight.'

So Markham confined himself to his room for a week, two weeks, three, while the monsoon rains swept across the hills, and a clinging mist gave everything a musty, rotting smell. By mid-August, life in a hill station can become quite depressing for its residents. The absence of sunshine has something to do with it. Even strolling along the Mall is not much fun when a thin, cloying drizzle is drifting into your face. No wonder some take to drink. The hotel bar had a few more customers than usual, although the carpet stank of mildew and rats' urine.

Markham made friends with a shrew that used to visit his room. Shrews have poor eyesight and are easily caught and killed. But as they are supposed to bring good fortune, they were left alone by the hotel staff. Markham was grateful for a little company, and fed his shrew biscuits and dry bread. It moved about his room quite freely and slept in the bottom drawer of his dressing table. Unlike the cat, it had no objection to Markham's face or lack of it.

Towards the end of August, when there was still no relief from the endless rain and cloying mist, Markham grew restless again. He made one brief, nocturnal visit to the park behind the hotel, and came back soaked to the skin. It seemed a pointless exercise, tramping through the long, leech-infested grass. What he really longed for was to touch that piano again. Bits of old music ran through his head. He wanted to pick out a few tunes on that cracked old instrument in the deserted ballroom.

The rain was thundering down on the corrugated tin roofs. There had been a power failure—common enough on nights like this—and most of the town, including the hotel, had been plunged into darkness. There was no need of mask or cape. No need for his false nose, either. Only in the occasional flashes of lightning could you see his torn and ravaged countenance.

Markham slipped out of his room and made his way

through the cellars beneath the ballroom. It was a veritable jungle down there. No longer used as a wine cellar, the complex was really a storeroom for old and rotting furniture, rusty old boilers from another age, broken garden urns, even a chipped and mutilated statue of Cupid. It had stood in the garden in former times; but recently the town municipal committee had objected to it as being un-Indian and obscene, and so it had been banished to the cellar.

That had been several years ago, and since then no one had been down into the cellars. It was Markham's short cut to the living world above.

It had stopped raining, and a sliver of moon shone through the clouds. There were still no lights in the hotel. But Markham was used to darkness. He slipped into the ballroom and approached the old piano.

He sat there for half an hour, strumming out old tunes.

There was one old favourite that kept coming back to him, and he played it again and again, recalling the words as he went along.

Oh, pale dispenser of my joys and pains,
Holding the doors of Heaven and of Hell,
How the hot blood rushed wildly through the veins
Beneath your touch, until you waved farewell.

The words of Laurence Hope's Kashmiri love song took him

back to happier times when life seemed full of possibilities. And when he came to the end of the song, he felt his loss even more passionately:

> Pale bands, pink-tipped, like lotus buds that float
> On these cool waters where we used to dwell,
> I would rather have felt you round my throat
> Crushing out life, than waving me farewell!

He had loved and been loved once. But that had been a long, long time ago. Pale hands he'd loved, beside the Shalimar…

He stopped playing. All was still.

Should he return to his room now, and keep his promise to Negi? But then again, no one was likely to be around on a night like this, reasoned Markham; and he had no intention of entering any of the rooms. Through the glass doors at the other end of the ballroom he could see a faint glow, as of a firefly in the darkness. He moved towards the light, as a moth to a flame. It was the chowkidar's lantern. He lay asleep on an old sofa, from which the stuffing was protruding.

Markham's was a normal mind, handicapped by a physical abnormality. But how long can a mind remain normal in such circumstances?

Markham took the chowkidar's lamp and advanced into the lobby. Moth-eaten stag heads stared down at him from the walls. They had been shot about a hundred years ago, when the hunting of animals had been in fashion. The taxidermist's art had given them a semblance of their former nobility; but time had taken its toll. A mounted panther's head had lost its glass eyes. Even so, thought Markham wryly, its head is in better shape than mine!

The door of the barroom opened to a gentle pressure. The bartender had been tippling on the quiet and had neglected to close the door properly. Markham placed the lamp on a table and looked up at the bottles arrayed in front of him. Some foreign wines, sherries and vermouth. Rum, gin and vodka. He'd never been much of a drinker; drink went to his head rather too quickly, he'd always know that. But the bottles certainly looked attractive and he felt in need of some sustenance, he poured himself a generous peg of whisky and drank it neat. A warm glow spread through his body. He felt a little better about himself. Life could be made tolerable if he had more frequent access to the bar!

Pacing about in her room on the floor above, Mrs Khanna heard a noise downstairs. She had always suspected the bartender, Ram Lal, of helping himself to liquor on the quiet. After ten o'clock, his gait was unsteady, and in the mornings he often turned up rather groggy and unshaven. Well, she was going to catch him red-handed tonight!

Markham sat on a bar stool with his back to the swing

doors. Mrs Khanna, entering on tiptoe, could only make out the outline of a man's figure pouring himself a drink.

The wind in the passage muffled the sound of Mrs Khanna's approach. And anyway, Markham's mind was far away, in the distant Shalimar Bagh where hands, pink-tipped, touched his lips and cheeks, his face yet undespoiled.

'Ram Lal!' hissed Mrs Khanna, intent on scaring the bartender out of his wits. 'Having a good time again?'

Markham was startled, but he did not lose his head. He did not turn immediately.

'I'm not Ram Lal, Mrs Khanna,' said Markham quietly. 'Just one of your guests. An old resident, in fact. You've seen me around before. My face was badly injured a long time ago. I'm not very nice to look at. But there's nothing to be afraid of. I'm quite normal, you know.'

Markham got up slowly. He held his cape up to his face and began moving slowly towards the swing doors. But Mrs Khanna was having none of it. She reached out and snatched at the cape. In the flickering lamplight she stared into that dreadful face. She opened her mouth to scream.

But Markham did not want to hear her screams again. They shattered the stillness and beauty of the night. There was nothing beautiful about a woman's screams—especially Mrs Khanna's.

He reached out for his tormentor and grabbed her by the

throat. He wanted to stop her screaming, that was all. But he had strong hands. Struggling, the pair of them knocked over a chair and fell against the table.

'Quite normal, Mrs Khanna,' he said, again and again, his voice ascending. 'I'm quite normal!'

Her legs slid down beneath a bar stool. Still he held on, squeezing, pressing. All those years of frustration were in that grip. Crushing out life and waving it farewell!

Involuntarily, she flung out an arm and knocked over the lamp. Markham released his grip; she fell heavily to the carpet. A rivulet of burning oil sped across the floor and set fire to the hem of her nightgown. But Mrs Khanna was now oblivious to what was happening. The flames took hold of a curtain and ran up towards the wooden ceiling.

Markham picked up a jug of water and threw it on the flames. It made no difference. Horrified, he dashed through the swing doors and called for help. The chowkidar stirred sluggishly and called out: '*Khabardar*! Who goes there?' He saw a red glow in the bar, rubbed his eyes in consternation and began looking for his lamp. He did not really need one. Bright flames were leaping out of the French windows.

'Fire!' shouted the chowkidar, and ran for help.

The old hotel, with its timbered floors and ceilings, oaken beams and staircases, mahogany and rosewood furniture, was a veritable tinderbox. By the time the chowkidar could summon help, the fire had spread to the dining room and was licking its way up the stairs to the first-floor rooms.

Markham had already ascended the staircase and was pounding on doors, shouting, 'Get up, get up! Fire below!' He ran to the far end of the corridor, where Negi had his room, and pounded on the door with his fists until Negi woke up.

'The hotel's on fire!' shouted Markham, and ran back the way he had come. There was little more that he could do.

Some of the hotel staff were now rushing about with buckets of water, but the stairs and landing were ablaze, and those living on the first floor had to retreat to the servants' entrance, where a flight of stone steps led down to the tennis courts. Here they gathered, looking on in awe and consternation as the fire spread rapidly through the main building, showing itself at the windows as it went along. The small group on the tennis courts was soon joined by outsiders, for bad news spreads as fast as a good fire, and the townsfolk were not long in turning up.

Markham emerged on the roof and stood there for some time, while the fire ran through the Empire Hotel, crackling vigorously and lighting up the sky. The people below spotted him on the roof, and waved and shouted to him to come down. Smoke billowed around him, and then he disappeared from view.

◆

When Darkness Falls

It was a fire to remember. The town hadn't seen anything like it since the Abbey School had gone up in flames forty years earlier, and only the older residents could remember that one. Negi and the hotel staff could only watch helplessly as the fire raged—through the old timbered building, consuming all that stood in its way. Everyone was out of the building except Mrs Khanna, and as yet no one had any idea as to what had happened to her.

Towards morning it began raining heavily again, and this finally quenched the fire; but by then the buildings had been gutted, and the Empire Hotel, that had stood protectively over the town for over a hundred years, was no more.

Mrs Khanna's charred body was recovered from the ruins. A telegram was sent to Mr Khanna in Geneva, and phone calls were made to sundry relatives and insurance offices. Negi was very much in charge.

When the initial confusion was over, Negi remembered Markham and walked around to the rear of the gutted building and down the cellar steps. The basement and the cellar had escaped the worst of the fire, but they were still full of smoke. Negi found Markham's door open.

Markham was stretched out on his bed. The empty bottle of sleeping tablets on the bedside table told its own story; but it was more likely that he had suffocated from the smoke.

Markham's artificial nose lay on the dressing table. Negi

picked it up and placed it on the dead man's poor face.

The hotel had gone, and with it Negi's livelihood. An old friend had gone too. An era had passed. But Negi was the sort who liked to tidy up afterwards.

A JOB WELL DONE

Dhuki, the gardener, was clearing up the weeds that grew in profusion around the old disused well. He was an old man, skinny and bent and spindly legged but he had always been like that. His strength lay in his wrists and in his long, tendril-like fingers. He looked as frail as a petunia but he had the tenacity of a vine.

'Are you going to cover the well?' I asked. I was eight, and a great favourite of Dhuki's. He had been the gardener long before my birth, had worked for my father until my father died and now worked for my mother and stepfather.

'I must cover it, I suppose,' said Dhuki. 'That's what the

Major Sahib wants. He'll be back any day and if he finds the well still uncovered he'll get into one of his raging fits and I'll be looking for another job!'

The 'Major Sahib' was my stepfather, Major Summerskill. A tall, hearty, back-slapping man, who liked polo and pig-sticking.

He was quite unlike my father. My father had always given me books to read. The Major said I would become a dreamer if I read too much and took the books away. I hated him and did not think much of my mother for marrying him.

'The boy's too soft,' I heard him tell my mother. 'I must see that he gets riding lessons.'

But before the riding lessons could be arranged the Major's regiment was ordered to Peshawar. Trouble was expected from some of the frontier tribes. He was away for about two months. Before leaving, he had left strict instructions for Dhuki to cover up the old well.

'Too damned dangerous having an open well in the middle of the garden,' my stepfather had said. 'Make sure that it's completely covered by the time I get back.'

Dhuki was loath to cover up the old well. It had been there for over fifty years, long before the house had been built. In its walls lived a colony of pigeons. Their soft cooing filled the garden with a lovely sound. And during the hot,

A Job Well Done

dry summer months, when taps ran dry, the well was always a dependable source of water. The bhisti still used it, filling his goatskin bag with the cool, clear water and sprinkling the paths around the house to keep the dust down.

Dhuki pleaded with my mother to let him leave the well uncovered.

'What will happen to the pigeons?' he asked.

'Oh, surely they can find another well,' said my mother. 'Do close it up soon, Dhuki. I don't want the sahib to come back and find that you haven't done anything about it.'

My mother seemed just a little bit afraid of the Major. How can we be afraid of those we love? It was a question that puzzled me then and puzzles me still.

The Major's absence made life pleasant again. I returned to my books, spent long hours in my favourite banyan tree, ate buckets of mangoes and dawdled in the garden talking to Dhuki.

Neither he nor I were looking forward to the Major's return. Dhuki had stayed on after my mother's second marriage only out of loyalty to her and affection for me. He had really been my father's man. But my mother had always appeared deceptively frail and helpless and most men, Major Summerskill included, felt protective towards her. She liked people who did things for her.

'Your father liked this well,' said Dhuki. 'He would often

sit here in the evenings with a book in which he made drawings of birds and flowers and insects.'

I remembered those drawings and I remembered how they had all been thrown away by the Major when he had moved into the house. Dhuki knew about it too. I didn't keep much from him.

'It's a sad business closing this well,' said Dhuki again. 'Only a fool or a drunkard is likely to fall into it.'

But he had made his preparations. Planks of sal wood, bricks and cement were neatly piled up around the well.

'Tomorrow,' said Dhuki. 'Tomorrow I will do it. Not today. Let the birds remain for one more day. In the morning, baba, you can help me drive the birds from the well.'

On the day my stepfather was expected back, my mother hired a tonga and went to the bazaar to do some shopping. Only a few people had cars in those days. Even colonels went about in tongas. Now, a clerk finds it beneath his dignity to sit in one.

As the Major was not expected before evening, I decided I would make full use of my last free morning. I took all my favourite books and stored them away in an outhouse where I could come for then from time to time. Then, my pockets bursting with mangoes, I climbed up the banyan tree. It was the darkest and coolest place on a hot day in June.

From behind the screen of leaves that concealed me, I

A Job Well Done

could see Dhuki moving about near the well. He appeared to be most unwilling to get on with the job of covering it up.

'Baba!' he called several times. But I did not feel like stirring from the banyan tree. Dhuki grasped a long plank of wood and placed it across one end of the well. He started hammering. From my vantage point in the banyan tree, he looked very bent and old.

A jingle of tonga bells and the squeak of unoiled wheels told me that a tonga was coming in at the gate. It was too early for my mother to be back. I peered through the thick, waxy leaves of the tree and nearly fell off my branch in surprise. It was my stepfather, the Major! He had arrived earlier than expected.

I did not come down from the tree. I had no intention of confronting my stepfather until my mother returned.

The Major had climbed down from the tonga and was watching his luggage being carried on to the verandah. He was red in the face and the ends of his handlebar moustache were stiff with Brilliantine. Dhuki approached with a half-hearted salaam.

'Ah, so there you are, you old scoundrel!' exclaimed the Major, trying to sound friendly and jocular. 'More jungle than garden, from what I can see. You're getting too old for this sort of work, Dhuki. Time to retire! And where's the memsahib?'

'Gone to the bazaar,' said Dhuki.

'And the boy?'

Dhuki shrugged. 'I have not seen the boy today, sahib.'

'Darin!' said the Major. 'A fine homecoming, this. Well, wake up the cook boy and tell him to get some sodas.'

'Cook boy's gone away,' said Dhuki.

'Well, I'll be double damned,' said the Major.

The tonga went away and the Major started pacing up and down the garden path. Then he saw Dhuki's unfinished work at the well. He grew purple in the face, strode across to the well, and started ranting at the old gardener.

Dhuki began making excuses. He said something about a shortage of bricks, the sickness of a niece, unsatisfactory cement, unfavourable weather, unfavourable gods. When none of this seemed to satisfy the Major, Dhuki began mumbling about something bubbling up from the bottom of the well and pointed down into its depths. The Major stepped on to the low parapet and looked down. Dhuki kept pointing. The Major leant over a little.

Dhuki's hand moved swiftly, like a conjurer making a pass. He did not actually push the Major. He appeared merely to tap him once on the bottom. I caught a glimpse of my stepfather's boots as he disappeared into the well. I couldn't help thinking of *Alice's Adventures in Wonderland*, of Alice disappearing down the rabbit hole.

A Job Well Done

There was a tremendous splash and the pigeons flew up, circling the well thrice before settling on the roof of the bungalow.

By lunchtime—or tiffin, as we called it then—Dhuki had the well covered over with the wooden planks.

'The Major will be pleased,' said my mother when she came home. 'It will be quite ready by evening, won't it, Dhuki?'

By evening the well had been completely bricked over. It was the fastest bit of work Dhuki had ever done.

Over the next few weeks, my mother's concern changed to anxiety, her anxiety to melancholy, and her melancholy to resignation. By being gay and high-spirited myself, I hope I did something to cheer her up. She had written to the colonel of the regiment and had been informed that the Major had gone home on leave a fortnight previously. Somewhere, in the vastness of India, the Major had disappeared.

It was easy enough to disappear and never be found. After seven months had passed without the Major turning up, it was presumed that one of two things must have happened. Either he had been murdered on the train and his corpse flung into a river; or, he had run away with a tribal girl and was living in some remote corner of the country.

Life had to carry on for the rest of us. The rains were over and the guava season was approaching.

My mother was receiving visits from a colonel of His Majesty's 32nd Foot. He was an elderly, easy-going, seemingly absent-minded man, who didn't get in the way at all but left slabs of chocolate lying around the house.

'A good sahib,' observed Dhuki as I stood beside him behind the bougainvillea, watching the colonel saunter up the verandah steps. 'See how well he wears his sola topi! It covers his head completely.'

'He's bald underneath,' I said.

'No matter. I think he will be all right.'

'And if he isn't,' I said, 'we can always open up the well again.'

Dhuki dropped the nozzle of the hose pipe and water gushed out over our feet. But he recovered quickly and taking me by the hand led me across to the old well now surmounted by a three-tiered cement platform which looked rather like a wedding cake.

'We must not forget our old well,' he said. 'Let us make it beautiful, baba. Some flower pots, perhaps.'

And together we fetched pots and decorated the covered well with ferns and geraniums. Everyone congratulated Dhuki on the fine job he'd done. My only regret was that the pigeons had gone away.

SUSANNA'S SEVEN HUSBANDS

Locally, the tomb was known as 'the grave of the seven-times married one'.

You'd be forgiven for thinking it was Bluebeard's grave; he was reputed to have killed several wives in turn because they showed undue curiosity about a locked room. But this was the tomb of Susanna Anna-Maria Yeates, and the inscription (most of it in Latin) stated that she was mourned by all who had benefited from her generosity, her beneficiaries having included various schools, orphanages and the church across the road. There was no sign of any other graves in the vicinity, and presumably her husbands had been interred in the old Rajpur graveyard, below the Delhi Ridge.

I was still in my teens when I first saw the ruins of what had once been a spacious and handsome mansion. Desolate and silent, its well-laid paths were overgrown with weeds, its flower-beds had disappeared under a growth of thorny jungle. The two-storeyed house had looked across the Grand Trunk Road. Now abandoned, feared and shunned, it stood encircled in mystery, reputedly the home of evil spirits.

Outside the gate, along the Grand Trunk Road, thousands of vehicles sped by—cars, trucks, buses, tractors, bullock-carts—but few noticed the old mansion or its mausoleum, set back as they were from the main road, hidden by mango, neem and peepul trees. One old and massive peepul tree grew out of the ruins of the house, strangling it much as its owner was said to have strangled one of her dispensable paramours.

As a much-married person with a quaint habit of disposing of her husbands, whenever she tired of them, Susanna's malignant spirit was said to haunt the deserted garden. I had examined the tomb, I had gazed upon the ruins, I had scrambled through shrubbery and overgrown rose-bushes, but I had not encountered the spirit of this mysterious woman. Perhaps, at the time, I was too pure and innocent to be targeted by malignant spirits. For, malignant she must have been, if the stories about her were true.

No one had been down into the vaults of the ruined mansion. They were said to be occupied by a family of cobras, traditional guardians of buried treasure. Had she really been a woman of great wealth, and could treasure still be buried there? I put these questions to Naushad, the furniture-maker, who had lived in the vicinity all his life, and whose father had made the furniture and fittings for this and other great houses in Old Delhi.

'Lady Susanna, as she was known, was much sought after for her wealth,' recalled Naushad. She was no miser, either. She spent freely, reigning in state in her palatial home, with many horses and carriages at her disposal. You see the stables there, behind the ruins? Now, they are occupied by bats and jackals. Every evening she rode through the Roshanara Gardens, the cynosure of all eyes, for she was beautiful as well as wealthy. Yes, all men sought her favours, and she could choose from the best of them. Many were fortune-hunters. She did not discourage them. Some found favour for a time, but she soon tired of them. None of her husbands enjoyed her wealth for very long!

'Today, no one enters those ruins, where once there was mirth and laughter. She was the zamindari lady, the owner of much land, and she administered her estate with a strong hand. She was kind if rents were paid when they fell due, but terrible if someone failed to pay.'

'Well, over fifty years have gone by since she was laid to rest, but still men speak of her with awe. Her spirit is restless, and it is said that she often visits the scenes of her former splendour. She has been seen walking through this gate, or riding in the gardens, or driving in her phaeton down the Rajpur road.'

'And, what happened to all those husbands?' I asked.

'Most of them died mysterious deaths. Even the doctors were baffled. Tomkins Sahib drank too much. The lady soon tired of him. A drunken husband is a burdensome creature, she was heard to say. He would have drunk himself to death, but she was an impatient woman and was anxious to replace him. You see those datura bushes growing wild in the grounds? They have always done well here.'

'Belladonna?' I suggested.

'That's right, huzoor. Introduced in the whisky-soda, they put him to sleep for ever.'

'She was quite humane in her way.'

'Oh, very humane, sir. She hated to see anyone suffer. One sahib, I don't know his name, drowned in the tank behind the house, where the water-lilies grew. But she made sure he was half-dead before he fell in. She had large, powerful hands, they said.'

'Why did she bother to marry them? Couldn't she just have had men friends?'

'Not in those days, dear sir. Respectable society would not have tolerated it. Neither in India nor in the West would it have been permitted.'

'She was born out of her time,' I remarked.

'True, sir. And remember, most of them were fortune-hunters. So, we need not waste too much pity on them.'

'*She* did not waste any.'

'She was without pity. Especially when she found out what they were really after. The snakes had a better chance of survival.'

'How did the other husbands take their leave of this world?'

'Well, the Colonel-sahib shot himself while cleaning his rifle. Purely an accident, huzoor. Although some say she had loaded his gun without his knowledge. Such was her reputation by now that she was suspected even when innocent. But she bought her way out of trouble. It was easy enough, if you were wealthy.'

'And, the fourth husband?'

'Oh, he died a natural death. There was a cholera epidemic that year, and he was carried off by the haija. Although, again, there were some who said that a good dose of arsenic produced the same symptoms! Anyway, it was cholera on the death certificate. And, the doctor who signed it was the next to marry her.'

'Being a doctor, he was probably quite careful about what he ate and drank.'

'He lasted about a year.'

'What happened?'

'He was bitten by a cobra.'

'Well, that was just bad luck, wasn't it? You could hardly blame it on Susanna.'

'No, huzoor, but the cobra was in his bedroom. It was coiled around the bed-post. And, when he undressed for the night, it struck! He was dead when Susanna came into the room an hour later. She had a way with snakes. She did not harm them and they never attacked her.'

'And, there were no antidotes in those days. Exit the doctor. Who was the sixth husband?'

'A handsome man. An indigo planter. He had gone bankrupt when the indigo trade came to an end. He was hoping to recover his fortune with the good lady's help. But our Susanna-mem, she did not believe in sharing her fortune with anyone.'

'How did she remove the indigo planter?'

'It was said that she lavished strong drink upon him, and when he lay helpless, she assisted him on the road we all have to take by pouring molten lead in his ears.'

'A painless death, I'm told.'

'But a terrible price to pay huzoor, simply because one

is no longer needed...'

We walked along the dusty highway, enjoying the evening breeze, and some time later we entered the Roshanara Gardens, in those days Delhi's most popular and fashionable meeting place.

'You have told me how six of her husbands died, Naushad. I thought there were seven?'

'Ah, a gallant young magistrate, who perished right here, huzoor. They were driving through the park after dark when the lady's carriage was attacked by brigands. In defending her, the gallant young man received a fatal sword wound.'

'Not the lady's fault, Naushad.'

'No, my friend. But he was a magistrate, remember, and the assailants, one of whose relatives had been convicted by him, were out for revenge. Oddly enough, though, two of the men were given employment by the lady Susanna at a later date. You may draw your own conclusions.'

'And, were there others?'

'Not husbands. But an adventurer, a soldier of fortune came along. He found her treasure, they say. He lies buried with it, in the cellars of the ruined house. His bones lie scattered there, among gold and silver and precious jewels. The cobras guard them still! But how he perished was a mystery, and remains so till this day.'

'What happened to Susanna?'

'She lived to a good old age, as you know. If she paid for her crimes, it wasn't in this life! As you know, she had no children. But she started an orphanage and gave generously to the poor and to various schools and institutions, including a home for widows. She died peacefully in her sleep.'

'A merry widow,' I remarked. 'The Black Widow spider!'

Don't go looking for Susanna's tomb. It vanished some years ago, along with the ruins of her mansion. A smart new housing estate came up on the site, but not after several workmen and a contractor succumbed to snake bite! Occasionally, residents complain of a malignant ghost in their midst, who is given to flagging down cars, especially those driven by single men. There have been one or two mysterious disappearances. Ask anyone living along this stretch of the Delhi Ridge, and they'll tell you that's it's true.

And, after dusk, an old-fashioned horse and carriage can sometimes be seen driving through the Roshanara Gardens. Ignore it, my friend. Don't stop to answer any questions from the beautiful fair lady who smiles at you from behind lace curtains. She's still looking for a suitable husband.

RHODODENDRONS IN THE MIST

Blood-red, the fallen blossoms lay on the snow, even more striking when laid bare. On the trees they blended with the foliage. On the ground, on those patches of recent snow, they seemed to be bleeding.

It had been a harsh winter in the hills, and it was still snowing at the end of March. But this was flowering time for the rhododendron trees, and they blossomed in sun, snow or pelting rain. By mid-afternoon the hill station was shrouded in a heavy mist, and the trees stood out like ghostly sentinels.

The hill station wasn't Simla, where I had gone to school, or Mussoorie, where I was to settle later on. It was Dalhousie, a neglected and almost forgotten hill station in the western Himalaya. But Dalhousie had the best rhododendron trees, and they grew all over the mountain, showing off before the colourless oaks and drooping pines.

But I wasn't in Dalhousie for the rhododendrons. It was 1959, and the Dalai Lama had just fled from Tibet, seeking sanctuary in India. Thousands of his followers and fellow-Tibetans had fled with him, and these refugees had to be settled somewhere. Dalhousie, with its many empty houses, was ideal for this purpose, and a carpet-weaving centre had been set up on one of the estates. The Tibetans made beautiful rugs and carpets. I know nothing about carpet-weaving, but I was working for CARE, an American relief organization, and I had been sent to Dalhousie (with the approval of the Government of India) to assess the needs of the refugees.

This is not the story of my tryst with the Tibetans, although I did suffer greatly from drinking large quantities of butter tea, which travels very slowly down the gullet and feels like lead by the time it reaches your stomach. The carpet-weaving centre became a great success, and I went on to work for CARE for several years; but that's another story. Out of one experience came another experience, as often happens during our peregrinations on planet earth, and it was during my stay in Dalhousie that I had a strange and rather unsettling experience.

Rhododendrons in the Mist

I was staying at a small hotel which was quite empty as no one visited Dalhousie in those days and certainly not at the end of March. The hill station had been convenient for visitors from Lahore, but Partition had put an end to that.

◆

The hotel had a small garden, bare at this time of the year. But on the second day of my stay, returning from the carpet-weaving centre, I noticed that there was a gardener working on the flower beds, digging around and transplanting some seedlings. He looked up as I passed, and for a moment I thought I knew him. There was something familiar about his features—the slit eyes, the broad, flattened nose, the harelip—yes, the cleft lip was very noticeable—but he wasn't anyone I knew or had known, at least I didn't think so… He was just a likeness to someone I had seen somehow, somewhere else. It was a bit of a tease.

And it would have remained just that if he hadn't looked up and met my gaze.

A flood of recognition crossed his face. But then he looked away, almost as though he did not want to recognize me; or be recognized.

I passed him. It was curious, but it didn't bother me. We keep bumping into people who look slightly familiar. It is said that everyone has a double somewhere on this planet. I had yet to meet mine—God forbid!—but perhaps I was seeing someone else's double.

I was relaxing in the verandah later that evening, browsing through an old magazine, when the gardener passed me on his way to the garden shed to put away his tools. There was something about his walk that brought back an image from the past. He had a slight limp. And when he looked at me again, his harelip registered itself on my memory. And now I recognized him. And of course he knew me.

I was the man who'd caught him rifling through my landlady's cupboards and drawers in Dehradun, some three years previously. I had exposed him, reported him, suggested she dismiss him; but the old lady, a widow, had grown quite fond of the youth, and had kept him in her service. He was good at running about and making himself useful, and, in spite of his cleft lip, he was not unattractive.

When I left Dehradun to take up my job in Delhi, I had forgotten the matter, almost forgotten the young man and my landlady; it was another tenant who informed me that the youth—his name was Sohan—had stabbed the old lady and made off with the contents of her jewel case and other valuables. She had died in hospital a few days later.

Sohan hadn't been caught. He had obviously left the town and taken to the hills or a large city. The police had made sporadic attempts to locate him, but as time passed the case lost its urgency. The victim was not a person of importance. The criminal was a stranger, a shadowy figure of no known background.

But here he was three years later, staring me in the face. What was I to do about him? Or what was he to do about me?

◆

After Sohan had gone to his quarters, somewhere behind the hotel, I went in search of the manager. I would tell him what I knew and together we could decide on a course of action. But he had gone to a marriage and would be back late. The hotel was in charge of the cook who, a little drunk, served dinner in a hurry and retired to his quarters. 'Don't you have a night-watchman?' I asked him before he took off. 'Yes, of course,' he replied, 'Sohan, the gardener. He's the chowkidar too!'

An early retirement seemed the best thing all round, especially as I had to leave the next day. So I went to my room and made sure all the doors and windows were locked. I pushed the inside bolts all the way. I made sure the antiquated window frames were locked. As I peered out of the window, I noticed that a heavy mist had descended on the hillside.

The trees stood out like ghostly apparitions, here and there a rhododendron glowing like the embers of a small fire. Then darkness enveloped the hillside. I felt cold, and wondered how much of it was fear.

I went to the bathroom and bolted the back door. Now no one could get in. Even so, I felt uneasy. Sohan was still a fugitive from the law, I had recognized him, and I was a threat to his freedom. He had killed once—perhaps more than once—and he could kill again.

I read for some time, then put out the light and tried to sleep. From a distance came the strains of music from a wedding band. Someone knocked on the door. I switched on the light and looked at my watch. It was only 10.00 p.m. Perhaps the manager had returned.

There was another knock, and I went to the door and was about to open it when some childhood words of warning from my grandmother came to mind: 'Never open the door unless you know who's there!'

'Who's there?' I called.

No answer. Just another knock.

'Who's there?' I called again.

There was a cough, a double-rap on the door.

'I'm sleeping,' I said. 'Come in the morning.' And I returned to my bed. The knocking continued but I ignored it, and after some time the person went away.

I slept a little. A couple of hours must have passed when I was woken by further knocking. But it did not come from the door. It was above me, high up on the wall. I'd forgotten there was a skylight.

I switched on the light and looked up. A face was outlined against the glass of the skylight. I could make out the flat rounded face and the harelip. It appeared to be grinning at me—rather like the disembodied head of the Cheshire cat in *Alice in Wonderland*.

The skylight was very small and I knew he couldn't crawl through the opening. But he could show me a knife—and that was what he did. It was a small clasp knife and he held it between his teeth as he peered down at me. I felt very vulnerable on the bed. So I switched off the light and moved to an old sofa at the far end of the room, where I couldn't be seen. There didn't seem to be any point in shouting for help. So I just sat there, waiting… And presumably, without a sound, he slipped away, and I remained on the sofa until the first glimmer of dawn penetrated the drawn window curtains.

◆

The manager was apologetic. 'You should have rung the bell,' he said, 'someone would have come.'

'The bell doesn't work. And someone did come…'

'I'm sorry, I'm sorry. The fellow's a villain, no doubt about it. And he's missing this morning. Your presence here must have frightened him off. So he's wanted for theft and murder. Well, we shall inform the police. Perhaps they can pick him up before he leaves the town.'

And we did inform the police. But Sohan had already taken off. The milkman had seen him boarding the early morning bus to Pathankot.

Pathankot was a busy little town on the plain below Dehradun. From there one road goes to Jammu, another to Dharamsala, a narrow-gauge railway to Kangra, and the main railway to Amritsar or Delhi. Sohan could have taken any of those routes. And no one was going to go looking for him. A police alert would be put out—a mere formality. He wasn't on their list of current criminals.

That afternoon I took a taxi to Pathankot and whiled away the evening at the railway station. My train, an overnight express to Delhi, left at 8.00 p.m. There was no rush at that time of the year. I had a first-class compartment to myself.

In those days our trains were somewhat different from what they are today. A first, second or third class compartment was usually a single carriage, or bogey. We did not have corridor trains. Bogeys were connected by steel couplings, otherwise you were not connected in any way to the other compartments. But there was an emergency cord above the upper berths, and if you pulled it, the train might stop. There were always troublemakers on the trains, just as there are today, and sometimes the chain was pulled out of mischief. As a result it was often ignored.

As the train began moving out of the station I went to all the windows and made sure that they were fastened. Then I bolted the carriage door. I was becoming adept at bolting doors and windows. Sohan was probably hiding out in some distant town or village, but I wasn't taking any chances.

The train gathered speed. The lights of Pathankot receded as we plunged into a dark and moonless night. I had a pillow and a blanket with me, and I stretched out on one of the bunks and tried to think about pleasant things such as scarlet geraniums, fragrant sweet peas and the beautiful Nimmi, star of the silver screen; but instead I kept seeing the grinning face of a young man with a harelip. All the same, I drifted into sleep. The rocking movement of the carriage, the rhythm of the wheels on the rails, have always had a soothing effect on my nerves. I sleep well in trains and rocking chairs.

But not that night.

I woke to the sound of that familiar tapping; not at the door, but on the window glass not far from my head. The insistent tapping of someone who wanted to get in.

It was common enough for ticketless travellers to hang on to the carriage of a moving train, in the hope that someone would let them in. But they usually chose the crowded second or third-class compartments; a first-class traveller, often alone, was unlikely to let in a stranger who might well turn out to be a train robber.

I raised my head from my pillow, and there he was, clinging to the fast-moving train, his face pressed to the glass, his harelip revealing part of a broken tooth… I pulled down the shutters, blotting out his face. But, agile as a cat, he moved to the next window, the sneer still on his face. I pulled down that shutter too.

I pulled down all the shutters on his side of the carriage. He couldn't get in, bodily. But mentally, he was all over me.

Mind over matter. Well, I could apply my mind too. I shut my eyes and willed my tormentor to fall off the train!

No one fell off the train (at least no one was reported to have done so), but presently we slowed to a gradual stop and, when I pulled up the shutters of the window, I saw that we were at a station. Jalandhar, I think. The platform was brightly lit and there was no sign of Sohan. He must have jumped off the train as it slowed down. It was about one in the morning. A vendor brought me a welcome glass of hot tea, and life returned to normal.

Rhododendrons in the Mist

◆

I did not see Sohan in the years that followed. Or rather, I saw many Sohans. For two or three years I was pursued by my 'familiar'. Wherever I went—and my work took me to different parts of the country—I found myself encountering young men with harelips and a menacing look. Pure imagination, of course. He had every reason to stay as far from me as possible.

Gradually, the 'sightings' died down. Young men with harelips became extremely rare. Perhaps they were all going in for corrective surgery.

The years passed, and I had forgotten my familiar. I had given up my job in Delhi and moved to the hills. I was a moderately successful writer, and a familiar figure on Mussoorie's Mall Road. Sometimes other writers came to see me, in my cottage under the deodars. One of them invited me to have dinner with him at the old Regal hotel, where he was staying. Before dinner, he took me to the bar for a drink.

'What will you have, whisky or vodka?'

No one seemed to drink anything else. I asked for some dark rum, and the barman went off in search of a bottle. When he returned and began pouring my drink, I noticed something slightly familiar about his features, his stance. He was almost bald, and he had a grey, drooping moustache which concealed most of his upper lip. He glanced at me and our eyes met. There was no sign of recognition. He smiled politely as he poured my drink. No, it definitely wasn't Sohan. He was too refined, for one thing. And he went about his duties without another glance in my direction.

Dinner over, I thanked my writer friend for his hospitality, and took the long walk home to my cottage. It was a dark, moonless night. No one followed me, no one came tapping on my bedroom window.

◆

Mussoorie had its charms. In my mind, every hill station is symbolized by a particular tree, even if it's not the dominant one. Dalhousie has its rhododendrons, Simla its deodars, Kasauli its pines and Mussoorie its horse chestnuts. The monkeys would do their best to destroy the chestnuts, but I would collect those that were whole and plant them in people's gardens, whether they wanted them or not. The horse chestnut is a lovely tree to look at, even if you can't do anything with it!

My walks took me to the Regal from time to time, and occasionally I would relax in the bar, chatting to an old resident or a casual visitor, while the barman poured me a rum and soda. He never looked twice at me. And I never saw him outside that barroom. He appeared to be as much of a fixture as the moth-eaten antler-head on the wall, only he wasn't quite as moth-eaten.

'Efficient chap,' said Colonel Bhushan indicating the barman. 'And a great favourite with his mistress.'

'You mean the owner of this place?' I had only a vague idea of who owned what in the town. And in some cases the ownership was rather vague. But in the case of the Regal— Mrs Kapoor, a wealthy widow in her fifties, was very much in charge, all too visible an owner; well fleshed-out, amplebosomed, with arms like rolling pins. Her staff trembled at her approach; but not, it seemed, the bartender, who led a charmed life, incapable of doing any wrong.

The lights went out, as they frequently do in this technological age, and the barman brought over our next round of drinks by candlelight.

By the light of a candle I caught a glimpse of the barman's features as he hovered over me. There was only the hint of a harelip, and the candle lit up his slanting eyes and prominent cheekbones. This was the only time I had a really close look at him.

◆

A week later I met Colonel Bhushan on the Mall. This was where all the gossip took place.

'Have you heard what happened last night at the Regal?' He wasted no time in getting to the news of the day.

A twinge of fear, of anticipation, ran through me. 'Nothing too terrible, I hope?'

'That barman chap—always thought he was a bit too smooth—stabbed the old lady, stabbed her two or three times, then plundered her room and made off with jewellery worth lakhs—as well as all the cash he could find!'

'How's the lady?'

'She'll survive. Tough old buffalo. But the rascal got away. By now he must be in Sirmur, or even across the Nepal border. Probably belongs to some criminal tribe.'

Yes, I thought, possibly a descendant of one of those robber gangs who harassed pilgrims on their way to the sacred shrines, or plundered traders from Tibet, or caravans to Samarkand… To rob and plunder still runs in the blood of the most harmless looking people.

So the barman at the Regal was the same man I'd known in Dehradun and then encountered in Dalhousie. The passing of time had altered his features but not his way of life. By now he would probably be far from Mussoorie. But I had a feeling I'd see him again—if not here, then somewhere else. Each one of us had a 'familiar'—a presence we would rather do without—an unwelcome and menacing guest—and for me it is Sohan.

Where does he come from, where does he go? I doubt if I shall ever know.

But I have a feeling he'll turn up again one of these days. And then?

A MUSSOORIE MYSTERY

Conan Doyle, the creator of Sherlock Holmes, had a lifelong interest in unusual criminal cases, and his friends often passed on to him interesting accounts of crime and detection from around the world. It was in this way that he learnt of the strange death of Miss Frances Garnett-Orme in the Indian hill-station of Mussoorie. Here was a murder combining the weird borders of the occult with a crime mystery as inexplicable as any devised by Doyle himself.

In April 1912 (shortly before the Titanic went down) Conan Doyle received a letter from his Sussex neighbour Rudyard Kipling:

A Mussoorie Mystery

Dear Doyle,

There has been a murder in India... A murder by suggestion at Mussoorie, which is one of the most curious things in its line on record.

Everything that is improbable and on the face of it impossible is in this case.

Kipling had received details of the case from a friend working in the Allahabad *Pioneer*, a paper for which, as a young man, he had worked in the 1880s. Urging Doyle to pursue the story, Kipling concluded: 'The psychology alone is beyond description.'

Doyle was indeed interested to hear more, for India had furnished him with material in the past, as in *The Sign of Four* and several short stories. Kipling, too, had turned to crime and detection in his early stories of Strickland of the Indian Police. The two writers got together and discussed the case, which was indeed a fascinating affair.

The scene was set in Mussoorie, a popular hill-station in the foothills of the Himalayas. It wasn't as grand as Simla (where the Viceroy and his entourage went) but it was a charming and convivial place, with a number of hotels and boarding-houses, a small military cantonment and several private schools for European children.

It was during the summer 'season' of 1911 that Miss

Frances Garnett-Orme came to stay in Mussoorie, taking a suite at the Savoy, a popular resort hotel. On 28 July she celebrated her 49th birthday. She was the daughter of George Garnett-Orme, of Skipton-in-Craven in Yorkshire, a district registrar of the Country Court. It was a family important enough to be counted among the landed gentry. Her father had died in 1892.

She came out to India in 1893 with the intention of marrying Jack Grant of the United Provinces Police. But he died in 1894 and she went back to England. Upset by his death following so soon after her father's, she turned to spiritualism in the hope of communicating with him. We must remember that spiritualism was all the rage in the early years of the century, seances and table-rappings being part of the social scene both in England and India. Madam Blavatsky, the chief exponent of spiritualism, was probably at the height of her popularity around this time; she spent her 'seasons' in neighbouring Simla, where she had many followers.

Miss Garnett-Orme's life was unsettled. She was drawn back to India, returning in 1901 to live in Lucknow, the regional capital of the United Provinces. She was still in contact with Jack Grant's family and saw his brother occasionally. The summer of 1907 was spent at Nainital, a hill-station popular with Lucknow residents. It was here that she met Miss Eva Mountstephen, who was working as a governess.

Eva Mountstephen, too, had an interest in spiritualism. It appears that she had actually told several of her friends about this time that she had learnt (in the course of a séance) that in 1911 she would come into a great deal of money.

We are told that there was something sinister about Miss Mountstephen. She specialized in crystal-gazing, and what she saw in the glass often took a violent form. Her 'control', that is her connection in the spirit world, was a dead friend named Mrs Winter.

As a result of their common interest in the occult, Miss Garnett-Orme took on the younger woman as a companion when she returned to Lucknow in the winter. There they settled down together. But the summers were spent at one of the various hill-stations. Was there a latent lesbianism in their relationship? It was a restless, rootless life, but they were held together by the strong and heady influence of the séance table and the crystal ball. Miss Garnett-Orme's indifferent health also made her dependent on the younger woman.

In the summer of 1911, the couple went up to Mussoorie, probably the most frivolous of hill-stations, where 'seasonal' love affairs were almost the order of the day. They took rooms in the Savoy. Electricity had yet to reach Mussoorie, and it was still the age of candelabras and gas-lit streets. Every house had a grand piano. If you didn't go out to a ball, you sang or danced at home. But Miss Garnett-Orme's spiritual pursuits took precedence over these more mundane entertainments. Towards the end of the 'season', on 12 September, Miss Mountstephen returned to Lucknow to pack up their household for a move to Jhansi, where they planned to spend the winter.

On the morning of 19 September, while Miss Mountstephen was still away, Miss Garnett-Orme was found dead in her bed. The door was locked from the inside. On her bedside table was a glass. She was positioned on the bed as though laid out by a nurse or undertaker.

Because of these puzzling circumstances, Major Birdwood of the Indian Medical Service (who was the Civil Surgeon in Mussoorie) was called in. He decided to hold an autopsy. It was discovered that Miss Garnett-Orme had been poisoned with prussic acid.

Prussic acid is a quick-acting poison, and would have killed too quickly for the victim to have composed herself in the way she was found. An ayah told the police that she had seen someone (she could not tell whether it was a man or a woman) slipping away through a large skylight and escaping over the roof.

Hill-stations are hotbeds of rumour and intrigue, and

of course the gossips had a field day. Miss Garnett-Orme suffered from dyspepsia and was always dosing herself from a large bottle of Sodium Bicarbonate, which was regularly refilled. It was alleged that the bottle had been tampered with, that an unknown white powder had been added. Her doctor was questioned thoroughly. They even questioned a touring mind-reader, Mr Alfred Capper, who claimed that Miss Mountstephen had hurried from a room rather than have her mind read!

After several weeks the police arrested Miss Mountstephen. Although she had a convincing alibi (due to her absence in Jhansi) the police sought to prove that some kind of sinister influence had been exerted on Miss Garnett-Orme to take her medicine at a particular time. Thus, through suggestion, the murderer could kill and yet be away at the time of death. In her first novel, *The Mysterious Affair at Styles* (1920), the poisoner was in a distant place by the time her victim reached the fatal dose, the poison having precipitated to the bottom of the mixture. Perhaps Miss Christie read accounts of the Garnett-Orme case in the British press. Even the motive was similar.

But there was no Hercule Poirot in Mussoorie, and in court this theory could never be made convincing. The police case was never strong (they would have done better to have followed the ayah's lead), and it appears that they only acted because there was considerable ill-feeling in Mussoorie against Miss Mountstephen.

When the trial came up at Allahabad in March 1912, it caused a sensation. Murder by remote-control was something new in the annals of crime. But after hearing many days of evidence about the ladies' way of life, about crystal-gazing and premonitions of death, the court found Miss Mountstephen innocent. The Chief Justice, in delivering his verdict, remarked that the true circumstances of Miss Garnett-Orme's death would probably never be known. And he was right.

Miss Mountstephen applied for probate of her friend's will. But the Garnett-Orme family in England sent out her brother, Mr Hunter Garnett-Orme, to contest it. The case went in favour of Mr Garnett-Orme. The District Judge (W.D. Burkitt) turned down Miss Mountstephen's application on grounds of 'fraud and undue influence in connection with spiritualism and crystal gazing'. She went in appeal to the Allahabad High Court, but the Lower Court's decision was upheld.

Miss Mountstephen returned to England. We do not know her state of mind, but if she was innocent, she must have been a deeply embittered woman. Miss Garnett-Orme's doctor lost his flourishing practice in Mussoorie and left the country too. There were rumours that he and Miss

Mountstephen had conspired to get hold of Miss Garnett-Orme's considerable fortune.

There was one more puzzling feature of the case. Mr Charles Jackson, a painter friend of many of those involved, had died suddenly, apparently of cholera, two months after Miss Garnett-Orme's mysterious death. The police took an interest in his sudden demise. When he was exhumed on 23 December, the body was found to be in a perfect state of preservation. He had died of arsenic poisoning.

Murder or suicide? This puzzle, too, was never resolved. Was there a connection with Miss Garnett-Orme's death? That too we shall never know. Had Conan Doyle taken up Kipling's suggestion and involved himself in the case (as he had done in so many others in England), perhaps the outcome would have been different.

As it is, we can only make our own conjectures.